Smoke from Distant Fires

Smoke from Distant Fires

An Historical Fiction

Doris Gaines Rapp

Daniel's House Publishing

Copyright © 2014 Doris Gaines Rapp

This book is a work of historical-fiction.
Mildred Marie Bryson Gaines was my mother. She really lived in
Randolph County, Indiana and was fourteen years old in 1925. Refer
to the Notes Section at the end of the book for comments regarding
the *fictional* part of the book. The *historical* information regarding
Tecumseh and his brother, the Prophet, is documented in history
books of Darke County, Ohio. See the Reference Section at the end
for further study of the county.

**Daniel's House Publishing
P.O. Box 623
Huntington, Indiana 46750**

Because of the dynamic nature of the Internet, any web addresses or
links contained in this book may have changed since publication and
may no longer be valid.

The cover art is a drawing of the Prophet sketched by the author.
Other similar images that were found online were without a proper
copyright notice and could not be used.

The photo on the back cover is of school friends: Bernice Whitecre,
Grace Stuckey, and Mildred "Millie" Bryson, taken 9/04/1925. No
resemblance to any friends in Millie's childhood is intended.

Cover elements assembled by The Type Galley, Warren, Indiana

Library of Congress Control Number: 2014934057
ISBN: 978-0-9637200-9-2 (sc)
ISBN: 978-0-9915033-0-8 (iBook)

Table of Contents

Dedication

This book is dedicated to all those who have distant ancestors. That would be all of us, my friend. You cannot change who they were, or who you were yesterday. You can only choose to live today — as if tomorrow mattered.

Doris Gaines Rapp

Acknowledgement

Thanks to my sweet husband, Bill. You are very supportive, loving and patient with all the hours I spend with my computer on my lap. Our life together has been a marvelous journey I plan to enjoy for many years to come. Like I have said, you have carried my books since I was eighteen years old. You continue to carry them with a smile on your face.

Thank you to Victoria Borgman for going over the manuscript and chasing down details that had been overlooked. I always read what I know I wrote, not what is written on the page. Thanks so much!

Many thanks to Debbie Wilson for your suggestions and support. You are a gifted author and editor, and better yet, a good friend.

A big thank you to the women who work in the Genealogy area of the Greenville (Ohio) Public Library. You were so helpful in my research of the early residents of Darke County.

Thank you also to the ladies at the Darke County, Ohio Court House. You were not only helpful you were willing to toss those huge books around for me. The County is blessed to have you.

I also thank the dear people who are in the writing group I attend. Your talent, honesty, encouragement and friendship are priceless. Thank you.

A big thank you to Debi Lindhorst at The Type Galley in Warren, Indiana for taking my cover pieces and creatively assembling them into a book cover.

To all my readers, I cannot express my thanks enough for your interest and positive feedback. Your comments have been so precious to me. Thanks again.

Introduction

Millie Bryson didn't know much about American Indians in 1925. At fourteen years old, she didn't know that acceptance, diversity, tolerance or empowerment, and Native Americans should have been spoken in the same sentence. In her little Indiana farming community, the only Indians she knew were the ones who thundered across the screen at the theater in Greenville, Ohio. In the movies, the settlers were "good" and the Indians were "bad."

A classroom assignment pushed her into a face-to-face experience with the first two new ideas. She had a lot to learn about the great, diverse people in God's world. That was where the fourth word came in – empowerment. She needed a healthy dose of empowerment to be able to do the research and fulfill the task that was given to her.

Millie was an independent girl who ventured out to wherever she chose to go. But, when her teacher gave the class an assignment that would reveal some of her family's history, she didn't feel brave at all. She just wanted to run, or hide, or become invisible, whichever was possible.

If she did the work, which she always did, others might call her names. Maybe, she wasn't as strong as she thought she was. If she didn't stand up for her own family, she would be no different than those who might taunt her.

Millie learned some important lessons from her assignment. She learned to accept all of who she was and to not forget the stories her grandparents told while she sat at their feet. She also learned to accept her ancestors and know they are part of who she is. Who she becomes is up to her.

As Old Grandfather would ask: Where stood your wigwams? Where sat your people? What are the stories they have told? We are each different, and we owe that to our ancestors.

Read the Notes section at the end of the book for a better understanding of the times in the United States in 1925. Pay close attention to the words with an asterisk (*) behind them.

1

Shadows from the Past

Millie Bryson stretched out her legs under her desk and tried to stifle a yawn. Normally, she loved her literature class. Her teacher would often read passages from the text book. She could make Millie cry by reading the dictionary.

"Stop it," Millie whispered into her hand, hoping to direct the sound behind her to where Steven sat. He had leaned forward and was using two pencils as drum sticks, tapping out a beat on the back of her head.

"Steven Lawrence, settle down. If I have to drive all the way out to your farm to talk to your father, I will." Miss Hollander slammed the book down on the desk as she looked up from Longfellow's *The Song of Hiawatha*. With her round, black schoolmarm glasses in her hand, she rubbed her eyes.

Millie straightened a little, casually reached back, and grabbed one of the pencils. She whipped it around in front of her and looked over at her friend Silvia, who sighed and rolled her eyes. Just at lunch, they had wondered if the boys in their school would ever grow up. In spite of Silvia's belief that they simply had to mature sometime, Millie couldn't see it happening any time soon.

It was nearing the end of class. School days in 1925* ended early in the afternoon. The boys needed those afternoon hours of daylight to work in the fields before supper. Harvest season had arrived in Indiana, in spite of a light snow that had started to fall after lunch. The long work hours led to sleepy eyes, short tempers, and a lack of concentration.

The school bell couldn't ring too soon for Millie, as she tried to muffle another yawn. She clenched her teeth, felt her ears ring and her eyes water.

Miss Hollander started to put her glasses back on and then stopped. "Mildred Bryson, be sure to see me after school, please."

"Yes, Ma'am." Millie tried to hide by sliding down in her seat. *Great, why did she have to remind everyone that my name is Mildred? I had almost completely trained everyone to call me Millie. Now she brings up that stuffy, old fashion Mildred name again. How do I live down that humiliation?*

She brushed a stubborn brown wave from her marcelled hairdo and glanced at Silvia. Her friend made a face like her lips had turned into a draw-string purse. Millie nodded and closed her eyes.

The entire eighth-grade English class squirmed in their seats as the sun sent glancing blows of light through the tall, schoolhouse windows. "Okay, where were we?" the teacher questioned, as she picked up the book that had stubbornly closed when she plopped it down.

"Part 1, Miss Hollander," Silvia Wagoner offered from the second seat, first row.

"Oh, yes, thanks, Silvia. Let's see," the teacher began again. "The people had been warned what might happen, if they didn't stop all the bloodshed and fighting. They had been given all that they needed, but they would not stop their dissensions."

Herbert Schmidt interrupted. "The Indians fought about everything," he grumbled with haughty superiority. "They were savages."

"You don't know anything about Indians," Silvia snapped back and folded her arms fiercely across her desk. She dropped her chin down on top of them.

"You mean that you do?" Herbert shot back as he pointed his finger in her direction. "Are you an Indian lover?"

"And why not?" Millie asked. "What's wrong with liking Indians?" She felt better. She could support her friend, while putting Herbert Schmidt in his place.

"I don't believe this," he stuttered.

"Well, I guess you're off the hook, Steven. It looks like I'll be visiting the Schmidt farm this evening." Miss Hollander picked up the book again. "Let's at least finish part one, before the school day is over."

Herbert slumped down in his seat as far as his hips could hold him before he slipped onto the floor. He closed his eyes and pouted.

"Close your eyes if you want to, Mr. Schmidt. Your ears are still open." Miss Hollander opened the book, put her wise-owl glasses back on, straightened her back and finished reading the portion of Longfellow she had intended for the day.

"I will send a Prophet to you,
A Deliverer of the nations,
Who shall guide you and shall teach you,
Who shall toil and suffer with you.
If you listen to his counsels,
You will multiply and prosper;
If his warnings pass unheeded,
You will fade away and perish!"[1]

"Now . . . ." Miss Hollander took a deep breath as she looked around at the class. Some of the students sat on the edge of their seats, while others looked like statues with faces of indifference or anger. "Due to the events of the afternoon, I have decided on a new assignment."

"Thanks, Herbert," Steven growled. "We are all going to be punished because you're a jerk*."

"You will not call anyone a derogatory name in my classroom, Mr. Lawrence. Let's see, your family's farm is two lanes down from Mr. Schmidt's place."

Like an after-thought she said, "Before I go on, Silvia, I'd like to speak to you, along with Mildred, for a moment after class." She removed her glasses, and folded them in her hand.

"What did we do?" Silvia gulped as she sat up stiffly, her eyes wide.

Millie's mouth dropped open as she glanced quickly at her friend. Now Silvia was singled out too!

"No, dear, you two didn't do anything. I just have a slightly different assignment for each of you." The teacher stood and came around to the front of her large wooden desk. Partially sitting on the edge, she leaned against it, crossed her low, black laced-up shoes, and relaxed. The corners of her mouth turned up, evidence that she was finding pleasure in the new assignment.

"The bell will ring in five minutes, Miss Hollander," Millie offered, always careful to obey the rules. Her mind raced. *Maybe Miss Hollander thought I was pestering Steven, not the other way around. But, what did Silvia do?*

"Thank you, Millie," she responded with a smile. She began slowly; her words were measured carefully. "Class, I am a little surprised by some of you. Your rejection of the American Indians and misunderstanding of the people in this area before the settlers came is discouraging. In order to increase your knowledge of the time of the pioneers and the indigenous people who lived here, I am giving you a research and writing assignment."

"I understand already," Herbert responded angrily. "I don't need a research paper. Some of my ancestors were killed by the Shawnee Indians who lived here."

Millie shot back. "Any family that has lived in Indiana for a long time has had members who were killed in the Indian Wars. That's a fact of history."

She looked over at Silvia who had folded her hands over her face, leaned over, and had curled up on her desk. What was wrong with her? She looked like she had wrapped herself into a tiny package.

Miss Hollander began again. "I realize there are painful memories on both sides, Herbert. The tribes of this area lost a lot of their people, as well as the settlers. Still, the assignment will be a five page paper from the view point of the Indians who lived here, including the Shawnee. While the Shawnee was not one of the five peaceful tribes, they played a large part in the conflict at the time. You will each present a five-minute speech after the research has been completed. Then, the final paper will be due two weeks later, before the two day Thanksgiving vacation."

"What?" Herbert was so stunned he nearly leaped out of his seat. "Five pages? It's harvest time!"

"Five pages aren't as bad as they could be if you don't stop complaining, Herbert." Millie whispered, shook her head, and looked from Silvia to her friend Sarah. "Can anyone control his mouth, since he isn't going to?"

"Miss Hollander, why are we being punished for what he did?" Silvia shook her head in disbelief.

"Herbert," Millie pronounced the "t" like she had hammered his name to the barn door. "Sit down!"

"Don't fret, Herbert," Miss Hollander said as she smiled. "I will talk with your father about your work schedule. Perhaps he'll let you work on your paper on Sundays. I know I haven't given homework to be done on the weekends in the past. But, if that is the only time you can work on it . . . well, don't worry." She looked around at the whole class. "If I have to, I'll talk to all of your families after church when the congregation gathers for cookies and punch. I'll see them then. All of you go to Bartonia Church." She eyed Herbert with the calm, but steely gaze, of one who has been used to winning an argument with a student.

"But . . ." Herbert began to protest.

"Shut up, Herbie!" Steven laughed. "It's your big mouth that gave us this paper."

"It's Bartonie," Millie corrected.

"I know that's how the community pronounces it. But, it's spelled, and correctly pronounced, Bartonia." Miss Hollander smiled.

The final bell of the day rang. Millie wished she could be the first one out of the classroom. But she had to stay and she didn't even know why.

Herbie wasted no time. It was obvious, he wanted out of there as he charted a straight path to the door.

"You're free to go, Mr. Schmidt," Miss Hollander called after him. "Just don't forget to begin the paper. The speech is due right before Thanksgiving. Let's try to be thankful that we have an opportunity to understand a part of history a little better."

· · · · ·

Millie went into the cloak room and waited impatiently. *Maybe Miss Hollander found out that I wrote Steven's history paper for him. Well, that shouldn't be a problem. He wrote it first and then I recopied it so she could read it.* She thought of every minor detail of her life as an eighth-grader.

"Thank you for staying after school, girls," Miss Hollander said, as the last of the students left the classroom. "I know that the hack* will be leaving soon. I told Steven to ask the driver to wait."

The girls looked at each other as they pulled their coats from wooden hangers. Millie shrugged in surrender to her teacher's superior authority.

"If you will, I'd like for you two girls to have a slightly different assignment." Miss Hollander eyed them carefully. "Millie, a prophet was sent to the Shawnee people. His name was actually *the Prophet*. He was buried in your great-great-grandfather's orchard. I thought your paper could be about him. I'd like to know more about that, and I think the class would too."

Millie tossed her thick waves, like a bolting thoroughbred horse. She was ready to run! "No, Ma'am!" she protested with wide eyes. "That isn't right! I would have known." Her face seemed to drain of color, fast. She wadded her already wrinkled cotton dress in her hand and felt wobbly as she grabbed a nearby desk.

Now, her humiliation was complete. She would be the laughing stock of the school. Her teacher called her by her formal name. That was bad enough. How would she ever live down this final disgrace? She would be called an Indian-lover for the rest of her life. Why would her teacher give her classmates the ammunition to hunt her down with another attack of teasing and mocking?

"Oh, Millie, I thought you knew," Miss Hollander apologized. "Most families know their ancestors and their family stories."

Millie tried to catch her breath. "Which grandfather was he?" Her voice was hoarse and strained.

"Your Ohio grandfather, James Bryson. He was an early settler of Darke County." Miss Hollander whispered, "Millie, Ohio is just a few miles down the Greenville Pike."

"Bryson," Millie smiled sheepishly. "Daddy is a very quiet person." She laughed, as she wiped some tears from her eyes. "He would not have talked much about him, because he doesn't talk very much about anything."

"Well, that is the assignment," the teacher stated and shrugged, as if she could do nothing about the Indian paper. Some phantom teacher must have made the assignment, not Miss Hollander.

Then the teacher turned to the other girl who waited for her fate, with an expression of terror. "And Silvia, I know that you are part Shawnee. So, I would like your assignment to be to tell us about your ancestry."

"What?" Millie gasped. "I have known Silvia Wagoner since the first grade." She had never even dreamed her friend might be an Indian.

Silvia threw her hands to her face as if she were trying to hide. "No one knows, Miss Hollander," she finally choked out a whisper. Her face was drawn tight in worry and her cheeks were red.

"I am sorry that both of you girls have had a shock this afternoon." Miss Hollander placed her hands on each girl's shoulder. "It is not a disgrace. You both have a heritage to be proud of."

"I didn't want anyone to notice me before," Millie protested. "Now, everyone will be looking at me."

"My dear, I have seen you stand up for others many times, but you won't stand up for yourself. Remember what the Bible says, when someone hurls arrows at you, speak back to them in truth, righteousness and peace."[2] Miss Hollander looked at Millie with a comforting smile.

"Righteousness?" Millie questioned.

"When something is morally right or just . . . you can be brave and speak up."

"I don't know . . . what if—" Millie stammered as she tried to think fast enough to come up with an alternative paper.

"Well, I do know," Miss Hollander summed up. "You two will have the most interesting papers of them all. I am sure of it."

Millie buttoned up her coat, numbly gathered up her books and stumbled out of Room 201. It was settled. She shook her head in disbelief. She had never even thought about her ancestors. Now, there were great-great grandparents and Indians on their farm. She turned and waited for Silvia to catch up to her. She was close behind.

"Do you believe this?" Millie whispered and looked over her shoulder to see if Miss Hollander would be able to hear her. "I don't want to work hard just so others can tease me."

"I know. Me either. But, Millie, you won't be harassed as much as I will. You're not an Indian. You're not Shawnee. I am."

"No, I'm a Shawnee-lover." Millie laughed and took Silvia's arm as they headed out of the school.

"Well, thank you very much, Millie. I like you too." Silvia laughed.

"We might as well laugh about it," Millie chuckled. "Besides, laughing won't give us a headache."

2

Harmony Crabtree

Millie burst out of the east door of the red brick Spartanburg School and skipped a few steps to get over the thin icy puddles that were under her feet. The sleet and snow that had started earlier in the afternoon had let up a little but continued to fall.

The school parking lot was a curious mix of old and new. The gravel portion of the lot was packed hard with tiny pebbles, sand, and farm topsoil carried into the school yard on high-top work shoes with leather laces, and scuffed brown oxfords. The students, who parked their Model T's there, carried remnants from the farm on the underbelly of everything that touched the ground.

The other half of the parking lot was earthen, or mud, depending on the season. Little tufts of grass were dotted here and there where the horses, still hitched to their buggies or wagons, waited tethered to hitching posts. Each of the hitches had a short-handled, black shovel hanging at one end of the upright post, above an old metal bucket. The buggy drivers, male or female, were responsible for cleaning up after their own animal. Millie watched one of the girls scoop up horse droppings with the shovel and plop the paddy in the bucket. She wasn't fond of the task — the flies, swishing tails, or twitching ears.

Millie called over to Silvia who boarded a different bus. "See you at the game tonight." Then, she caught up with Stephen and matched his pace, step for step. "There will be a pre-season basketball game this evening," Millie mouthed breathlessly as the early snow fluttered and fell. Her frozen breath remained suspended around her head like a great crystalline halo.

"Right," Stephen agreed, then followed her onto the shiny, yellow school bus that was parked out front beside the school.

As usual, Herbert Schmidt had run ahead of everyone, just like any small child, and had positioned himself as the official door opener. He always stood with one foot in the stair well and the other foot on the floor of the bus. Hunched over, he could lean on the metal handle that operated the door. Millie figured he saw himself as the bus conductor. How did he attain that position of power? His grandfather was the bus driver.

Millie often wondered how she could love the crotchety, old Mr. Schmidt, and loath his infantile grandson. But it was a fact not worth debating at that point. She could barely brush past the chubby Herbert when she boarded the bus. He did not let that go unnoticed.

"Gaining weight are you, Bryson?"

There again, was an accusation that would be nearly impossible to live down if others picked up on the taunt. Obviously, she had not put on a single pound. Her mother was a little alarmed about her skinny profile. So, she kept pushing milk in Millie's direction, even though she didn't like the warmish, unpasteurized cow-juice that came from the cooling water of the milk house.

"The bulging hips seem to be coming from our esteemed door-opener, not the passengers. Besides, polite Christians do not bring embarrassment to others." She turned up her nose at Herbert and made her way past the pesky nuisance at the door.

"What's God going to do? Strike me down?" Childish Schmidt mocked.

Millie ignored the last comment and found a seat in the back of the bus and settled down. She stared out the window that quickly frosted over with the warmth of her breath.

"You gonna pull that skirt out of the way, or am I supposed to sit on it?" Stephen snickered as he started to sit down.

"There are other seats, Stephen Lawrence. You can sit anywhere," she said with a little smile.

"Maybe I want to sit with you, sassy girl," he teased. Stephen swung his body onto the cushion, and then ran his fingers over the back of the seat in front of them. "Isn't progress great, Millie? This thing is ritzy. It wasn't very long ago that we were riding to school on that old, horse-drawn hack. It was like a buggy with many seats. Not much better than an old bathtub." Stephen beamed with pride as he surveyed the new school bus.

"Sure," Millie murmured. "But, I kind of liked the old hack and the clop, clop of the horses' hooves on the hard dirt roads. It was a nice, slow, soothing ride home."

"*Slow* is right and dirt for the road is even more right. We're growing out here, Millie."

"I'm not ready to grow right now. Looks like I'm going to be stuck in the past for a while." She felt conflicted inside. She was curious about what she might find out about her distant ancestors and dreaded the outcome at the same time.

"Whoa!" Steven yelled when a Tin Lizzie* whizzed around the bus as it was slowing at the end of a farm lane.

Mr. Schmidt slammed on the breaks, which knocked the ever-present Herbert to the floor.

"Don't test God, Mr. Bus Conductor," Millie reminded him as she gathered up her books that had slid off her lap. She could not resist reprimanding the silly-soul that was now flat on the floor.

Sixty-five-year-old Mr. Schmidt stumbled, stepped widely over his grandson, and jumped down off the bus. Millie could see him run around the front of the vehicle and wave his fist in the air at the Model T that had just buzzed the bus.

"Slow down you, donkey," he yelled. "I'm driving children." He hiked up his pants, climbed back up the steps, pushed Herbert aside, sat down and put the bus in gear.

"What did you say a minute ago, Herbert?" Millie shouted. She sat back, with a satisfied smile on her face and lost herself in her own thoughts.

Grandpa James, why did you embarrass me so much? No one . . . and I mean, not a single soul, will let me live this down. How can I go back to hiding in the shadows after you've shone a spotlight on me?

Then she thought about Silvia and the ancestral skeleton in her closet. Her secret was even more deadly than her own. Silvia was the Indian no one was supposed to love . . . and she was her friend.

Millie jumped up from her thoughts. The bus had stopped in front of her home, a white frame farmhouse, on the road just a few miles down from Spartanburg High School, between Lynn and Bartonia.

"See you at the game tonight?" She didn't wait for an answer. Stephen was always there, at school, at afterschool activities, and at church. But she didn't know why he had to be such a tease.

She breezed past Herbert without so much as a, "See you tomorrow." He was lucky he hadn't said another word to her because she was in no mood for his nonsense. She wanted to think only of the upcoming game.

As Millie hurried up the lane to her house, she could feel the anticipation. It was Friday in Indiana and there was definitely a high school basketball game that evening. Millie could feel it. The excitement seemed to hang in the air like a snapshot of a scrambling, floating and well-executed rebound. There was nothing like Hoosier basketball to stir the enthusiasm of all the fans, young and old.

Basketball was even popular in the girls' physical education classes, where eighth-grade girls in knickers* bounded up and down the gym floor, with the black tie and sailor collar of their middy* flowing behind them. But only the boys played for the fans to cheer them on. The little high school basketball team provided a source of pride, fire and entertainment for the entire farm community.

Millie hurried along the long, rutted lane that led from the road to their farmhouse. Fresh sleet and snow peppered her cheeks and stuck to her nose.

I sure hope the game isn't canceled because of snow, she thought as she slid along on the icy gravel of the lane. Millie pulled her coat even more tightly around her, drew her felt, wide brimmed hat down low, and aimed her bent head toward the warmth that surely waited inside.

"Millie . . . oh Millie, dear." Harmony Crabtree had rolled down the window of her gray Pontiac sedan an inch, and had raised her chin to shout out the open crack. "Is your mother home?"

"Gee, Mrs. Crabtree," Millie stammered. She tried to be polite, while at the same time, she kept her back bent and her eyes fixed on the kitchen door. "I don't think so. It looks pretty gloomy with the snow and all. I don't see a light in the window."

"I'm sorry, Millie. Jump in the car and I'll drop you off at the door." Mrs. Crabtree leaned over, pulled down on the door handle and popped it open to the blowing snow. "Hurry, dear."

Millie was cold and getting colder, but she wasn't sure she wanted to talk to Harmony Crabtree badly enough to get in the car with her. Harmony was a member of the large brick church with the tall steeple, about three miles past the high school. She had been Bertha Bryson's friend since they were in grade school together as children. Bertha, Millie's mother, had learned to tolerate Harmony's ways, but, Millie had not developed that talent as yet. Millie was sure that tolerance must be a talent that one either has or doesn't have. It doesn't grow with you, like your shoe size.

"Harmony Crabtree is a fine Christian woman," Bertha had told Millie.

That statement only made Millie question whether she understood the meaning of being a Christian. Millie figured that God must have seen to it that the woman was named Harmony, since, in his infinite wisdom and ability to see through time, he was sure no harmony would flow from her, except for her given name.

Millie gave in to the weather and slid in on the cold seat of Mrs. Crabtree's Pontiac. As she sat in Harmony's car, she felt trapped again, just as she had in past encounters with the woman.

She felt so uncomfortable sitting there, she found herself holding her breath, waiting until she could get away from her. Harmony had a shrill, on-the-attack manner.

Harmony seemed to like Millie and her mother. She was always very kind to them. Or, perhaps, she just liked those she was with and slandered those she was not.

"I wanted to tell your mother what that preacher's wife said to me, just this afternoon." Harmony pursed her mouth, as if set in her own character assessment of Pastor Bennington's Rachel Rose.

"Mrs. Crabtree, please, I . . ." Millie did not want to hear another twisted truth, another near lie. But Harmony was without sympathy that day, as she had been on most other days.

Harmony began her offensive attack. "I saw the preacher's wife at the market this afternoon. I said, 'Wasn't that a lovely service on Sunday?' And she said, 'Yes, but the Sunday school classes are certainly disorganized, aren't they?'" Mrs. Crabtree puffed herself up like she was coming to a rolling boil. "The Sunday school classes? Can you believe it? I am the Sunday school superintendent at that church. How dare she!"

"Were they, Mrs. Crabtree?" Millie asked sweetly.

"Were they what?" Harmony blustered.

"Disorganized? I thought Mrs. Simpson and Mrs. Stringer's families were all quarantined with the measles. Don't those moms teach some of the classes at your church?" Millie's questions ran like syrup from her lips. Perhaps she was developing a talent after all.

"Well, yes, they are sick, but the preacher's wife had no business talking to me like that." Harmony stumbled over her words, as if they fell like boulders from her mouth.

"Let me help you, Mrs. Crabtree. Was that her exact word —disorganized?" Millie began to have fun with the conversation. If she could not get out of it, she might as well make a game of it.

"Yes, yes," Mrs. Crabtree stuttered. "She said, 'The Sunday school class schedule was disrupted today, Harmony. That's too bad.' Disruptive! Do you believe that?"

"Yes, Ma'am, but you said *disrupted* not *disruptive*." Millie enunciated the two words slowly and distinctly, emphasizing the difference in pronunciation and implied meaning. She felt herself warming up and wondered where the heat was coming from.

"Yes, dear, disruptive." Harmony Crabtree paused for a moment, a rare occurrence indeed. Then she added, "Well, you are quite young, dear. You tell your mother I was here and wanted to talk to her."

Millie wanted to protest, to make her point. Then, she smiled to herself. Actually, she had. It took a lot for Harmony Crabtree to become speechless.

3

Shadows in the Field

Millie bounded up the front steps of her parents' farmhouse, rounded the veranda and darted in through the kitchen door. Her mother didn't like her to come through the front door. The front door opened into the formal parlor with its matching chairs of maroon mohair velvet, blue glass top tables, leaded crystal vases and needlepoint pillow shams of festive colors and fancy work. That was only for company, both the door and the parlor.

Millie slipped off her galoshes and set them by the barnyard door on the little enclosed back porch. Buckets of fresh transparent pie apples that had been picked from the orchard a few days before waited to be tended to.

She put her schoolbooks on the tin-covered cabinet top, next to an empty butter crock, and swung her wool coat onto the coat rack that stood in the corner. She tossed her hat on top of it in one rhythmic motion, acquired from years of following the same routine — the hat, the coat, and then her instructions. She retrieved a small piece of paper that had been tucked in the frame of the backdoor window which led from the porch to the warm kitchen.

As Millie mechanically went about filling the teakettle from the pitcher pump at the sink, she glanced at the list of chores. She placed the kettle on the back burner of the big black, Home Comfort Range that commanded a presence in the middle of the kitchen. She took the small iron bar from its resting place on the back of the stove and slipped it into the little hole in the back iron burner, much like a crowbar would easily lift a manhole cover from a city street. She peered in and smiled. There appeared to be enough wood in the firebox of the cook stove to heat the kettle and begin supper. The burner began to glow under the teakettle.

Millie settled herself at the table, unfolded her black, round-rimmed glasses, which she hated, and put them on. The frames reminded her too much of Miss Hollander's specs, and she was old. She must have been at least twenty-seven.

She scanned the note for a moment and calculated the amount of time it would take to complete the chores. She wondered about Silvia's list. Her aunt and uncle demanded so much from her. Millie imagined her list probably included a bottom note about rebuilding the barn out of Herbert Schmidt's Lincoln Logs, or something else just as impossible.

Millie sighed and picked up the tally of her daily chores again. Her parents would be home soon. They had gone to Union City for groceries and supplies, according to the message. The list read the same as always:

1. Do your studies.
(Millie never had to be reminded to do her schoolwork. She was a very good student. But, her mother had written that instruction at the top of every after-school list since Millie was in the second grade, and she certainly was not going to stop the practice.)
2. Put the chicken in the pot with a little water. We will have chicken and dumplings for supper.
3. Run a dust rag over the living room.
4. Supper at 5:30
5. Basketball game at 7

Millie poured herself a cup of hot tea, sat back and stretched her legs across the chair beside her. She would not have dared sit so unladylike if her mother had been home. Mother expected proper posture at the kitchen table.

A spoonful of honey in her tea was just the thing to warm her insides and spur enough energy to accomplish her work. Millie ran her teaspoon round and round in the teacup, dissolving the sweet nectar from the hives that her father kept in the woods.

Scratch, rustle. What was that sound? She sat up straight and listened to the room. Nothing. The tea tasted warm and good as she drank it to the bottom of the cup. A second cup was not part of her usual after-school routine. Normally, she enjoyed just a few minutes of relaxation before she began her chores and homework. Today, with the chill, and Harmony Crabtree, it would be a two tea cup day.

The kettle sat on the warming burner at the back of the old stove. She reached for it and then stopped. There was that sound again. She didn't know whether to run out of the house, and back into the icy wind or . . . she couldn't think of an *"or."* She poured another cup of hot water for her tea.

What a silly girl you are. She shrugged off the nonsense of hearing sounds in the house. Old farm houses, like theirs, would have all kinds of noises. Wind could catch the curtains and flutter them a bit. In fact, the wind could whistle around the window panes, where the caulking could come loose and rattle the glass. And, everyone knew that old hardwood floors creak when you walk on them. Wait, toss that one out. That would mean someone else was in the house doing the walking. She didn't want to think about that.

Scrape. That was it. There was someone in the house. She knew it.

Millie grabbed Momma's meat cleaver from where it hung on a hook above the stove. As she retrieved it, the sound was louder and more familiar. It wasn't the sound of some*one*. It was noise of some*thing*.

She peered behind the stove and into the empty space where it stood away from the wall. The great cast iron range was warm all the way around. That was its attraction.

There, in a puddle of fur, lay Fussbudget, Millie's giant gray cat, and all four of her kittens. She must have dragged them in to find warmth from the cold. Momma had always said that cats belong in the barn.

Cats were just another farm animal. Their job was to catch barn mice. As a small child, Millie could go out to the barn to play with the cats, after she put on a pinafore to protect her dress. Momma did not want any cat hair or barn germs in the house.

Millie understood the *why* Fussbudget had gotten into the house. It was cold outside. That fall had been mild with sunny days and balmy nights. Then, they got up one morning to frigid temperatures and the first snow of the season. *How* she got in was a puzzle, a puzzle that would have to be solved another time. Right then, she had to get that mother cat and her kittens out of the house before Momma came home from town.

"Come on, Fussbudget," she smiled and coaxed at the cat. "Come on."

The cat didn't move. She just sat there, huddled over her kittens, with that looking-through-the-looking-glass stare that all cats have, at least all the cats that have lived in the Bryson barn.

An enticement was obviously needed. Millie hurried out to the back porch, pulled the broom from where it hung suspended between two nails, and marched back into the kitchen, fully armed. At first, she tried to pull at the great mound of fuzziness. That didn't work. She went around to the other side of the stove and pushed at them, like so much kitten dust. They moved all right. They scattered. They darted off in every direction possible for five cats, one large and four very small.

Those were not house cats, with a respect for interior furnishing and refinement. They were field and barn felines, and their wildness exploded all over the house. Some ran into the sitting room and one started to climb her mother's drapes. Those curtains had taken her mom two days to make, and weeks of egg money to purchase the fabric.

Millie cringed. "Get down off there," she shouted as she waved the broom in the air. One of them, the little male cat, darted up the stairs to who-knows-what-mischief. Millie didn't want to think about that.

She tried the gentle approach. "Here kitty, kitty," she purred. That certainly didn't work. If cats could laugh, she was sure they were enjoying her attempts at herding them. Then, she tried the cunning approach. She charged into the kitchen, opened the ice box, and took out a strip of bacon. She hoped her mother wouldn't miss just one. But then, of course, it wasn't her fault the cats had gotten in.

With the end of the strip of bacon firmly clutched in her right hand, she waved it around in circles above her head. It looked a little like a very short lariat preparing to lasso the beasts. The room began to fill with the scent and promise of bacon. All the cats circled around her legs and tried to leap high enough to win the prize. Millie moved toward the door, opened it wide and flung the bacon strip out in the yard past the porch. All five four-legged fur balls streaked out into the cold afternoon. She slammed the door quickly before the cats could come back in for a full bacon sandwich.

Millie stood at the door and watched the cats wrestle over the ownership of one little strip of pork. Then, she fixed her eyes on something in the barnyard, beyond the porch.

"What was that?" she choked. She looked again, but all she saw was the last of the fall leaves. Their colors provided a pretty contrast between the white snow and the oranges and reds. Soon, all of the leaves would be gone. She thought about how much she would miss the beauty outside when she was alone in the house, waiting for her parents to come in.

Millie walked over to the table and picked up her teacup. But, she didn't feel comfortable about something. She went back to the window and looked out on the yard where the light was casting long shadows across the lawn. She thought she had seen something out there and blinked once, sipped her peppermint tea and came back to the closed schoolbooks that sat before her. She reached toward them and then drew her hand back, as if she had been burned. What in the world was she going to do about Great-Great-Grandpa's Indian? She knew she was going to have to ask her father about his family. She didn't look forward to that.

It wasn't that Daddy didn't talk about his family. It was simply that Daddy didn't talk. He was a very quiet man, who worked hard from sunrise to sunset. He was also rather shy. He rarely cracked jokes, except for one. Whenever the season of tilling and planting came around in the spring, he would say, "Well, I'd better get out there. I've got a date with Allis." Of course, his Allis Chalmers tractor was the only love that waited for him in the field.

Leaves and twigs blew by the window again. It looked cold out there. Millie was glad she was inside. Suddenly, she heard the barn door bang. Daddy was so careful about keeping the door latched; she didn't see how it was possible for the door to catch the wind. Even if she stayed inside, she should at least check from the window. But, she was frozen in fear. All this talk about Indians made her uncomfortable. They had studied the great Indian wars in school. A lot of violence happened at that time in history.

Finally, she got up enough nerve to creep into the sitting room, where she could peer out the window from behind her mother's heavy drapes.

An Indian blanket of white and black flapped in the cold wind, around the shoulders of a man who kept getting closer to the house. Who was that? What could she do? Where could she hide?

She jumped in fright. Her heart pounded. The back kitchen door opened.

"Millie, where are you?" Someone called from the back porch.

Her eyes grew large as she tried to wrap herself in the curtains. She heard someone walk through the kitchen and stop at the sitting room door.

"Why didn't you bring in the blankets I had hung on the line? I wanted them to freshen up before the snow started?" Bertha Bryson stared at the girl who now unwrapped herself from the draperies. "What on earth are you doing?"

"I think I'm being haunted, Mother," she admitted as she ran her fingers over the curtains to straighten out any creases she may have caused.

"Fiddlesticks," her mother muttered as she took off her coat and hung it on the back of the chair to dry.

"But, Momma I saw . . ."

"Saw what?" Daddy questioned as he dumped the black and white blankets on the couch. Then he turned to Bertha, "These are still damp."

"Well, let's see . . . . Hang them on the line on the back porch. After dinner, we'll drape them over the back of some kitchen chairs where they can warm by the stove and finish drying." She turned to attend to the groceries in the kitchen. Then she asked, "What did you say that you saw?"

"Oh, never mind," Millie said as her hands dropped to her sides in relief. Then, with great dramatic emphasis, she threw the back of her hand to her forehead and whispered, "My ghosts have floated away on the autumn wind."

Bertha rolled her eyes and sighed, "That's nice, dear."

4

Indians at the Table

"Don't drop the chicken," Bertha cautioned with whispered intensity.

Millie used two large forks to lift the bird from the cooking pot. She watched it slip and flip over on the platter. They both gasped as it wobbled a little on the breast bone, and then finally landed, like a capsized ship, on its side.

"I just finished stirring the dumplings in time," Millie spoke to herself out loud. She dropped them in the pot of piping hot broth, while her mother ripped the meat from the bone of the bird and threw it back in the kettle. It became a rhythmic dance, dumpling, then meat and do-si-do.

They started laughing when Daddy came into the kitchen and called out, "Allemande left!"

Millie's eyes grew bright as she wiped dumpling flour on her apron. Daddy was in a good mood. He picked up the evening newspaper, placed his elbows on the table, and balanced the paper between them. She slowly put silverware at each place, as she thought of a way to bring up the topic of Miss Hollander's literature assignment. As she looked at the spoons and knives, she casually said, "I wonder what the Indians used for forks."

"Indians? You ask the strangest questions," her mother replied. Speaking for Raymond had become a habit, developed over many years of few words coming from his mouth.

"Spoons," he said without looking up from his paper.

"What?" Bertha was stunned. Raymond had spoken.

"Spoons," he said again as he folded his paper and placed it beside the plate. "They made spoons out of wood."

"Wood?" Bertha questioned again.

Millie looked from Daddy to Momma. What would be her mother's reaction to the thought of Indians invading their evening conversation?

"Sure . . . wood," he answered as he picked up his freshly poured cup of coffee.

"How do you know that?" Bertha questioned in disbelief.

"How do I know?" He smiled as he replaced the cup on its saucer. "You've seen the little box of arrowheads I keep on the shelf. I find them in the ground when I till the soil. I've found some small wooden spoons and forks too. They're in the same box."

"Well, I knew you had the arrowheads . . . ." Bertha stammered, "but, I hadn't seen the forks and stuff."

"Oh . . . maybe I didn't think to show them to you."

"You didn't think I would be interested?"

"In Indians?" he nearly choked on the coffee he held in his mouth. "You usually say, 'Shh Daddy*. Don't let others hear you talking about them.'"

"I do?" she said as she served him a large ladle full of the chicken and dumplings. She looked at Millie for confirmation.

"You do, Momma," she said matter-of-factly.

"Well, I'm sorry about that. A proper woman should accept everyone," she concluded with satisfaction as she sat down. "Let's pray."

Bertha always said grace at meals. Raymond was respectful, but did not lift up words of thanks, at least, not out loud. Millie often wondered if he talked to God out in the fields. She nearly choked when she heard her mother finish the prayer.

"And thank you Lord that someone got those cats out of my kitchen. They belong in the barn as you intended, Amen."

"You knew Fussbudget and her kittens were in the kitchen?" Millie gasped.

"Well, of course. They were under my feet while I fixed lunch."

"I found them and thought you'd be mad, so I got them out of the house with a piece of bacon."

"Well, that's a piece of bacon that won't land on your breakfast plate, but . . . that was a clever idea." She chuckled.

Millie felt relieved. She hoped her next question would be received as well as her cat-catching feat. "So . . . it would be all right, if our family were friends with Indians?" Millie launched phase two of her plan to get information about her distant grandfather.

"Friends with Indians?" her mother stopped and wiped her mouth on her napkin. "You are asking the strangest questions today!"

"Yes, Indians," Millie held her ground.

"There haven't been any Indians around here in years," her mother announced, as though her words would make it so.

"Yes, there are," Raymond threw in softly.

Bertha just stopped and stared at him. Raymond spoke so seldom, Bertha's practice had been to pause and listen to him.

"Where are they?" Millie asked, excited that he knew about the first settlers.

"Oh, there are a few around about," he said as he cleaned up his plate with a piece of his wife's homemade brown bread.

"Does our family know any?" she asked, inching toward the real questions.

"Well, there's a fellow up at the garage in Greenville who is part Shawnee."

"Who, what's his name?" Bertha snapped back.

"Well, now, that's a puzzle. If others know, his boss could lose business."

"Why?" Now that was a new twist Millie hadn't thought about. What were people afraid of? If the remaining Shawnee lived such quiet lives that no one knew who they were, they weren't a threat to anyone.

"People can be not very nice sometimes," her father answered. "Some people are so prejudiced they might refuse to trade where an Indian works."

"Speaking of 'not very nice,' Mother, Harmony Crabtree came by today to gossip about her pastor's wife."

"Millie Bryson!" her mother gulped and nearly inhaled her dessert applesauce.

"Well, she was, Mother. And, to my thinking, there is no harmony at all in Mrs. Crabtree. God must have been half-asleep when he handed out pleasant personalities."

"Don't you get the Lord involved in your storying," she warned her.

"I am not storying. It's the truth, Momma. She came by here to see you, so she could complain about Rachel Rose. And Rachel Rose was only misunderstood. Mrs. Anti-Harmony never has anything good to say about anyone," Millie announced.

"Harmony Crabtree is the best reason for not giving out names of people who could be fodder for Harmony to feed on," Raymond stated.

"Well, that's enough about Harmony Crabtree . . . and I don't want to hear you call her Anti-Harmony again, Millie," her mother said.

"Yes, Ma'am," she agreed. Then she paced herself for phase three.

"We're going to write papers about the Indians who lived around here, back in the early eighteen-hundreds," she began, choosing a safe approach, or at least, she hoped it was.

"Oh?" Bertha said no more.

"And, she wants me to take a slightly different approach."

"What's that?" her mother asked, not knowing what bear trap she was stepping into.

"She said that Tecumseh's brother, the Prophet, was buried on James Bryson's farm . . . Great-Great-Grandpa." Millie sat back and waited for the reaction to come.

"Oh, I don't think so," Bertha said calmly. "I'll talk to her at church on Sunday. She is mistaken."

"No, she isn't," Raymond corrected again.

Bertha was obviously flabbergasted. Her hands dropped into her lap, a sign of surrender to Millie's thinking. Neither Millie nor her mother said another word, as they waited for the new historian to continue.

"Some members of the family say it is true. Others don't want the story told."

"What about telling me, Daddy?" Millie asked, as she waited nervously for the answer. Her curiosity wanted to know, but she didn't want anyone else to know.

Visions of Harmony Crabtree dancing around a witch's cauldron, hand-in-hand with Herbert Schmidt, chanting, "Indian lover, Indian lover," popped into her mind. She shuddered at the image and tried to toss the picture as far as she could fling it.

"Well, Millie, like I always say," her mother said firmly, "tell the truth and do your homework. We can't pick and choose our assignments."

Millie's mouth flew open. But, she thought it was best to fill it with a forkful of chicken, rather than change her mother's mind by choosing the wrong words.

5

The Games

"You want to drive, Millie?" Daddy asked before he started the car later that evening.

"Raymond!" Bertha snapped. "She's fourteen years old. She doesn't even drive the tractor yet."

"Now is as good a time as any to start." He put the key in the ignition and waited.

"Well, not on a dark, windy, snowy night. I'll have to put my foot down on that." Bertha spoke with determination and folded her arms.

"That's okay, Daddy," Millie gave in quickly. "I don't know if I'll ever want to drive." She smiled to herself. "I would really like to ride a horse."

"A horse?" Bertha asked sharply.

Millie's mother had been driving for several years. She had talked to Millie many times about teaching her to drive.

"Let's save the driving or riding conversation for another day," Raymond suggested. The car grew peacefully quiet.

The shiny black T-model,* four-door Ford, pulled out of the barnyard and bounced onto the road. By the time they had turned toward the high school, it was decided. Millie's folks agreed to take her and some friends for an after-game treat, win or lose. Daddy had said so, and this was the day for Daddy to speak.

It was November, and the night had overtaken the day long before 7 p.m. Double dotted lights, from motor cars and buggies, approached the school from every direction. Carriage lanterns dimly glowed on buggies that had been brought back into use. That afternoon, as soon as the snowflakes began to drift down, sleigh rails were attached to old buggy frames, in place of the wheels, by some wise travelers.

At the school, the crisp air carried the sounds of happy basketball fans. They had battled Union City High School many times in previous years and anticipated another victory this time, even if it was a pre-season game. Their excitement started all the way out in the parking lot. Millie eagerly jumped from the car, the moment it stopped in the lot beside the gymnasium entrance. The snow had started to stick to the ground. It was getting slick.

In 1925, girls' skirts were scandalously hemmed an inch below the knee. Thank goodness coats were long and warm. She pulled hers even more closely around her small frame as she hurried toward the door.

Silvia waited for her, between the bitter cold of the outside world and the warmth of the gym, just inside the door. Silvia always seemed to be between, never quite here, but not there either. Ever since her father died, she had been caught between what she wanted to do and all the distorted requirements her aunt and uncle placed on her.

"Oh, I'm glad you're here alone," Silvia blurted out, as Millie stopped and braced herself against the blowing snow, so beautiful and yet so cold.

"You girls had better hurry on in," Millie's mother warned as she and her dad breezed past. "It's cold out here."

"We will," Silvia said, but tugged on the sleeve of Millie's coat to coax her to linger.

"Steven will probably show up, and I'm sure Sarah is here already. She always comes early and I'm usually late." Millie took Silvia's arm and tried to guide her into the brightly lit gym, where body heat alone would raise the temperature to a tolerable level.

"Wait, Millie." Silvia held her friend's arm in the frosty, biting cold. "It's so loud in there."

"Well, all right. But, can we step inside and find a quiet corner? My bloomers* are freezing." Millie danced from one foot to the other, as she tried to keep the blowing snow from waltzing up her skirt. Her coat was long but her skirt was short. Her gartered stockings stopped a few inches above the knee, leaving only skin between their rolled down tops and her short, white bloomers.

The girls blew in through the double doors on a frigid blast of north wind, and slipped around the corner in the direction of the science lab. The noise from gathering basketball fans, and the robust pep-band, clattered to a joyously ruckus volume. But, Silvia did not appear to be in a celebration mood. Stress had burned a cloud across her dark brow.

"Millie, I don't know if I can wait four more years until I can get out of here."

"What's wrong?" Millie's excitement about the game and possible win soon gave way to worry for her friend. She knew that Silvia had always been trapped between wishes and her reality.

Silvia pulled a handkerchief from her coat pocket and blotted the tears that had started to run down her cold cheeks. Finally, the words tumbled out, like children's blocks that had been shoved into a closet to make the room appear clean, when chaos was just beyond the closet door.

"Aunt Ida said I can't go with all of you after the game. I told her we were just going for ice cream. She said, 'Yes, but you didn't come in on time the last time.' I told her that Uncle Wilber said I could stay out 'til ten-thirty. And, she said, 'But, I told you ten.' And, I said, but you told me ten after I got home. How could I have known before that?'"

Silvia paused and cupped her hands over both ears, as if to block the continuing flurry of double messages that bombarded her every day.

"Slow down, Silvia." Millie put her arms around her friend and comforted her. "Maybe, if I ask your aunt for you. See?" Millie began.

"Would you, Millie? They're in the stands now." Silvia hugged her, as though Millie had just saved her life.

"I'll go in first and look around, so your aunt doesn't think we have cooked up a plot. You find Sarah, and I'll join you after I talk to your aunt." Millie shoved her gloves into her pockets, removed her coat, and carried it into the lively gym.

She scanned the gathering fans, and spotted Mr. and Mrs. Strausburger near the top of the stands. That was a lucky placement, since it would have been too noisy to talk to them if they were any nearer to the pep band. After she climbed the bleachers, row by row, she casually slipped in beside them.

"Good evening, Mr. and Mrs. Strausburger," Millie started politely. "I was just asking Silvia about joining the gang for ice cream after the game."

"Did she tell you to talk to me?" Mrs. Strausburger shot back.

"No, Ma'am. I volunteered." Millie tried to use sweetness and poise, to both calm and charm Silvia's aunt.

"She's just like her mother. Did you know that, Millie? Before she died, God rest her soul, I said that woman was crazy. She always had ideas of her own, always thought she was different. She even slept-in on Sunday mornings, and expected us to take Silvia to church."

Mrs. Strausburger's face never changed from its frozen, sour position. Millie thought her rigid expression was amazing. How could she hold the same scowl for hours — days even?

"Didn't she work long hours on Saturdays, after Silvia's dad was killed in the war?" Millie didn't want to sound impertinent.

What she really wanted to say was, "Gee Whiz — Silvia's mom stood on her feet, working for twelve hours on Saturdays. I would guess she would be so tired, her toes would curl up after all of that." But, she didn't say anything. She had learned when to make a point, and when the point was too sharp to make any point at all.

"Are you back-talkin' me, Millie?" The self-appointed-savior-attitude dripped from Ida Strausburger's tongue like venom, as she hissed out the well-rehearsed tale of Silvia's childhood.

"No, Ma'am. I was just trying to understand the circumstances."

"There are no circumstances other than . . . Sunday morning is for church. Only sinners and crazy folks, who want to do everything their own way, stay home. Silvia's mother always wanted to be different."

Without stopping to recoil, Aunt Ida slithered and slid into a second, unrelated attack. "Just like Elmer Winslow, over there on 600W. Everybody knows that his wife died of unhappiness. He'd never go to church with her either. Now, he's courtin' that maiden lady from Winchester, and goin' to that Ungodly Church with her."

Millie could feel her face grow hot with impatience. How could Silvia ever ask questions about her Shawnee ancestors, from this woman of ignorance and prejudice? She tried to remain calm and controlled, even though she could not control the words that fell from her lips.

"Mrs. Strausburger, Elmer Winslow is a physician. He was usually on call on Sunday, since old Doc Hamilton always had Sundays off. And, his wife died in childbirth. And . . . what Ungodly church are you talking about?"

Millie caught herself and realized that line of attack would not win some time away for Silvia. So, she added with some imagination, "I want to make sure I never attend that church, Mrs. Strausburger! Holy cow!"

Ida's piercing glance struck Millie sharply. "I don't remember the name of it, Millie. But, they believe that all people are basically good, and we know that only God is good, don't we, Millie?"

"Yes, Mrs. Strausburger. God is very good indeed. And . . . I know that He watches over all of the work you do for your church. I heard that you made all of the pies for the ice cream social last summer, and everyone said they were the best they'd ever eaten." Millie smiled sweetly, and then turned her eyes toward the gym floor for fear that staring into that woman's eyes any longer would surely cast a spell on her that would have long lasting, dire consequences. Like . . . her first born child could be carried away by an evil troll.

"Yes, they were good, Millie. You know the secret to great pies don't you?" She paused for effect, as Millie pretended to listen intently. "Don't over-work your crust, dear." Ida patted her hand, just like a loving great-aunt might do, as she passed on the family baking secrets to the next generation.

How does Silvia ever know who she's talking to? Dear Aunt Ida or Witch Ida from Freakishstan?

Without taking her eyes from the floor below, Millie responded sugary sweet. "Thank you, Mrs. Strausburger. I'll try that next time Mother wants a pie for supper. I always end up with a split pie crust that's so misshapen I have to re-roll it again. I'll try your baking secrets. And . . . ah, do you add corn starch or flour to thicken the fruit for the filling?"

"Corn starch, of course, Millie, dear. I wish Silvia was as interested in baking as you are," Ida cooed.

"I imagine she is, Mrs. Strausburger. She just doesn't want to mess up your kitchen. She knows what a good housekeeper you are." She was beginning to feel nauseated from the sweet pie and even sweeter talk.

"We won't be out late this evening," she continued. "Silvia should be home by eleven. Daddy and Mother are taking us to Uncle Henry's drug store for sodas. I know Uncle Henry doesn't want to get home late either. He'll have to open again, early in the morning. I hope Silvia can go with us," Millie held her smile and held her breath at the same time.

"Well, if you're sure she'll be home by eleven, Millie. Usually, I want her to be in by ten-thirty p.m. sharp. This one time, it should be all right if she gets home by eleven. Now, don't make this a habit, Millie Bryson." Ida put her arm around her and gave her a little hug. "I know Bertha raised you proper. Silvia has good friends."

"Oh, thank you, Mrs. Strausburger. Jeepers!" Millie threw her handkerchief over her mouth. "Excuse me. Mother doesn't like me to use coarse words." She bolted from her seat and started to bound down the stairs between the bleachers, then turned and threw in a little insurance. "We'll watch the time, and, thanks again for the baking tips. I'll use them for sure."

Near the gym floor, the pep-band was playing a rousing jitterbug, interspersed with the loyal school song and some crisp marching tunes. Sarah and Silvia waited for her in the student section. She was just in time for the tip-off.

"Where's Steven?" Sarah mouthed over the din of the band music and screaming fans.

"He's coming." Millie formed the words with her mouth, although no sound was heard. Then, she turned to Silvia with an impish gleam in her eye and mimed, "You are going for ice cream after the game. Be home by eleven, not ten-thirty like *usual*." She dragged the words out in exaggerated enunciation.

Silvia's mouth flew open and hung there like a mailbox door the rural carrier forgot to close. "Ten-thirty . . . as *usual*?" Silvia mouthed a scream and silently shouted again, "As usual!?"

"As usual," Millie whispered. Then she added, "But, eleven tonight, Silvia."

"Oh, that's jake*! Thank you," Silvia pantomimed and threw her arms around Millie's neck in relief.

"I'm here." Steven grinned broadly as he came up behind Millie in the bleachers, where she stood with her friends. "Can I get some of that huggin' too?" He threw his arms around the two girls in a great embrace. "You too, Sarah," he laughed, and drew her into the hug turned wrestling hold. Together, they all jumped up and down, until the girls had enough of Steven's grasp.

"Okay, okay, Steven," they all pleaded.

"Let loose, Steven. I'm crushed." Millie shouted as she smoothed her hair and then asked, "Why do you have to be so rough?" But, it was futile. The noise would not permit any conversation at the game. That was evident.

Both teams dashed up and down the floor in breathtaking plays. Even the fans in the stands seemed as lively and involved as the players. Dan Chaney coached his boys with spirit and fire, laced with old fashioned integrity and determination. Each team charged rapidly, with little or no pause or hesitancy, twisting, setting up, shooting, and showing that they came to win.

Tom Norman passed off to Eric Fiddler, who snapped the ball to Harvey Bergdorf. Harvey dribbled through the middle with Hoosier hoops ability and barn-yard grace, swung around behind the husky farm boy from Union City High, then, popped the ball back to Eric. Eric jumped, poised an elegant mid-air aim and sunk the basket. The final bell rang just as Fiddler's basketball shot hit the boards again. Score: Spartanburg 78, Union City 77.

6

Darke County, Ohio

"Are you going to Uncle Henry's for ice cream?" Millie asked Steven as she gathered up her belongings at the end of the game, which wasn't easy. Coats and hats and gloves had flown everywhere.

Steven had been her best friend, and worst enemy, since they were in Mrs. Byrd's second grade class. He would stuff paper wads down the back of her shirt whenever he was behind her. That evening, it was assumed that he would join them after the big game.

"Yep, I'm riding with Bruce Fiddler in Eric's truck. It'll be cold as ice back there, but we can take it. We're Spartan men!" He proudly showed his muscles. The energy generated from the game had him running at top speed. The excitement had not died down and neither had he.

"Just make sure you don't puff yourself up so much you bounce out of the back of the truck," Sarah teased.

The joyous, triumphant celebration started on the glistening hardwood floor of the little rural high school gym. Then, like a giant wave, the fans stormed the players with hugs, broad slaps on the back, and jubilant congratulations.

The excitement continued with uproarious laughter and a re-telling of each play, as the community swarmed out through the double doors and into the frosty night air. But no one was cold. They were completely unaware of the blistering wind that had picked up to a stiff swirl. The entire shouting throng piled into their cars and buggies and blasted their way out of the parking lot with horns blaring, shouts of laughter, and pumped up excitement. Millie, Sarah and Silvia were shoehorned into the back seat of the Bryson car.

The celebration wound and bounced across the state line, into the quaint Ohio town of Greenville. In the second business block, Millie's dad parked the Model T in front of the Greenville Drug Store. Eric pulled his truck into the space next to them. When the girls got out of the car, Millie nudged Silvia and gestured in the direction of the Darke County Court House, a block down on Broadway. "We need to get in there," she mouthed. Silvia nodded. It was both exciting and disappointing to be so close to their answers, and yet unable to get inside.

"Do they keep maps of the county and farmland in the Court House?" Millie asked her father as casually as she could. She wasn't ready to tell her parents about the assignment. She didn't know how they felt about the Bryson history and their connection to the Indians who had lived in the area. She never thought they would be ashamed. But, since they had never told her the story of Grandpa James' orchard, she could only guess they were embarrassed or afraid others wouldn't approve.

"The Court House?" Daddy said. "Well, I suppose. You know, you can probably get a lot of that kind of information at the library."

Millie stored that suggestion for later use. Somehow, they would get back to Greenville – when it was open. How they would get there, was too big of a hurdle to leap over that evening.

At that hour, the Palace Department Store, Murphy's Five and Dime and the rest of the stores were already closed. The drug store was the only establishment that was still open. Its bright lights made it sparkle, like a jewel in the middle of a necklace.

Henry Ledbetter, owner and pharmacist, was a great supporter of everything his niece, Millie, did. "Hi, Princess," he greeted as she and her friends blew in the door. "Your expression tells me you must have won!" Uncle Henry was a round, friendly soul with graying hair. He wore a white apron that covered his middle where the clothing took the greatest splatter and smears from fountain pens, chocolate sauce, or spilled cough syrup.

"Yes, we did!" Millie shouted.

"I've saved a booth for you and your friends. There's a *reserved* sign on it." He slapped Raymond on the shoulder and added, "There's another booth over there for you and Bertha. Gotta keep the driver happy," he laughed.

"Thanks, Gee Whiz, that's super!" Millie said as she and the girls slid onto the facing benches.

Like a spirited, wiggling puppy, Steven jumped into the seat beside her. He caught Henry's eye and shouted. "Giant banana split, please." Uncle Henry nodded.

"I'll have a chocolate soda," Millie ordered. The other two girls followed with matching requests.

"They'll be ready in a minute." Uncle Henry tapped his order pad and left to fill it. Even Aunt Helen had come in that evening to help fill all the orders.

"Okay girls," Steven grinned. "So . . . what did you think about the game?"

"You're joking, aren't you?" Sarah rolled her eyes and slapped the table.

"You can't say anything to bring me down tonight, Missy," he snapped back. "Harvey's been off his game all week. He's still upset over . . ." his eyes caught the menu and didn't complete his thought.

"Steven Lawrence, you've known what you were going to order all week. You just ordered it. Do you want more food?" She pulled playfully on his shirt sleeve and then asked. "What were you going to say? What's Harvey stewin' about?" Millie prodded.

"It's not for me to say," he said.

"But you will, of course." Silvia cleared her gloves from the table to make room for the ice cream concoction Uncle Henry placed in front of her.

"Since when do boys 'not say'? You boys are the biggest gossips in school!" Sarah accused him.

"We are not. Everyone knows that girls wag their tongues about others more than guys." He defended his brotherhood as he dug his spoon into the chocolate syrup end of the split. "I'm just saying it was good to see that Harvey was on top of his game again."

"Because he had been really down . . ." Millie prompted, "because . . .?" She sipped some of the soda through her straw and pretended she wasn't digging for more information.

"It's a family thing," he said.

"We all know families can be embarrassing," she encouraged. "Harvey's dad . . ."

"No, not his dad," Steven blurted out, "his uncle."

"His Uncle . . . Freddie . . .?" she suggested.

"Uncle George," he admitted.

"I'm so sorry to hear about it," Millie sympathized as she dipped her spoon into the ice cream floating in her soda. She took a bite and launched a new possibility. "They don't get stuff like this in jail."

"Who told you he was in jail?" Steven nearly choked on a piece of banana.

"You just did," Sarah laughed.

He slid down in the booth for a second, and then quickly revived with another spoonful of ice cream and pineapple syrup. "Harvey was worried that people would think he was dishonest too."

"People can be cruel," Silvia agreed, but said no more.

"What about prejudice? What if there was a scandal in your family's past? How would you live that down?" Millie asked casually. She didn't want too many questions in return.

"How is that possible, silly? Everybody knows everybody around here. If there is no secret, there is no scandal."

"Yes, but, what if there is something way back in the past, in a time that people alive now, wouldn't even know about?" She shook her head. "Why do people want to hurt others so much?"

"Who, Millie? What has changed? You weren't talking about scandal and people wanting to hurt others this morning on the bus?" he asked but kept on eating. "And, you sure had fun at the game."

"I don't know what's changed." She shooed off his question with a wave of her hand and another sip from her soda.

Silvia kept her eyes pinned to the bottom of her soda glass. She helped Millie out of the conversation by changing the subject. "This is the best soda I've had in a long time."

Steven scooped up the rest of his split and patted his stomach. "I could eat another one, but Eric is giving me the signal. He wants to go." He stood and put on his jacket.

"Say," he added, "I have an idea about that scandal stuff. I'd call the newspapers and give them the story, before anyone hears about it. Even dirty socks lose their smell when they're out in the fresh air."

· · · · · ·

"Morning's coming early tomorrow," Bertha warned the girls when they got into the car.

"Why tomorrow?" Sarah asked with a yawn.

"Not *just* tomorrow. She means we won't be able to get up in the morning. The yawn gives it away," Millie said with a wry smile.

"We'll all have to get up before the rooster crows. The chores will have to be done," Silvia added. "I know I have to be up at 5 a.m. to do the milking."

"You do the milking?" Sarah asked. "My dad and brothers do those chores."

"I don't have any brothers or a dad," she answered wistfully.

"Daddy does the milking; he and Mother plant, cultivate and harvest; and I fix dinner and take care of the house," Millie said as she tried to stifle another yawn. She covered her mouth and cleared her voice to make it sound as chipper as possible.

With her hand still over her mouth, she asked, "I was wondering . . . do you think we could drive past the old farm where Great-Great-Grandpa James lived?" She hoped she had sounded alert enough for another adventure, before they headed back to Indiana and bed.

"James?" Bertha questioned. "James Bryson?" She turned slightly in her seat to face her daughter. "Millie, what is this all about?"

"Just a writing assignment for our class," she faked a yawn and pretended to close her eyes, so she wouldn't have to answer too many more questions.

Backfire.

"You look too tired to me. Besides, I don't think Daddy knows where the farm is." She turned to Raymond. "Have you been to the old farm?"

"No, not really," he admitted. "I just know his farm was south of the city."

"Well, that settles it," her mother stated flatly. "We are going west, not south."

Millie sighed. She began to feel like she was going in all directions at the same time, and still didn't know where to begin or how to get there.

"You hadn't gone to the farm as a boy?" She pursued the thought just a bit more.

"We went to my Grandfather's farm, Morris Bryson, up in Woodington, Ohio, north of Greenville. We had great times there. He put up a huge swing in a big tree out back. We could swing so high it felt like we were flying." Raymond let the car bound over the country roads at just the right speed, that their stomachs were left suspended in the air.

"Why don't you ever talk about your childhood, Daddy?" Millie wondered out loud.

"I guess each day has its own joy. I think about my family. I'm sorry if I haven't talked about it."

"Daddy* doesn't talk very much" Bertha announced. "But, when he does, we try to listen carefully."

"But, James was his great-grandfather. He would have been your grandfather's father. Didn't he talk about his own grandfather?' Millie protested. If she had been more awake, she may not have pressed the issue as much as she did.

"All I remember is," he spoke slowly, "he was a farmer, a justice of the peace, a judge, and an Ohio Councilman. His wife was Rachel."

"Raymond," Bertha gasped. "You never told me that."

"Didn't I? Well . . . he was."

"Tell me more, Daddy," Millie pleaded. He might not be in a talkative mood again for a long time.

"His wife, my great-grandmother, was married before. Her first husband, Henry Rush, was killed by Indians at Fort Rush, in one of the Indian wars."

"Your great-grandmother had two husbands?" Millie couldn't believe it.

"Well, not at the same time." Her father adjusted his coat a little.

"Daddy," Bertha sputtered. "Don't say such a thing."

"Why not, Mother?" Millie asked. "Her husband died and she re-married. It's not like she was divorced."

"Divorced! I never want to hear you say such a thing again. Those are not our people." She pulled her handkerchief from her pocket and dabbled at her face.

"Well, they're mine," Millie whispered as she looked at Silvia and smiled. Sarah had already fallen asleep, but Millie thought she would have agreed.

Again the air floated beneath their bellies, until it fell on the other side of the road bump. It had been a very interesting, uplifting day.

7

Research

"I don't know how to start this paper," Millie whispered to Silvia on her way out of church on Sunday. "We had two weeks, but it's slipping away fast. We have to go to Ohio to get the information we need."

"Maybe we could get into Union City more easily than Greenville. We can look in the library right here in Indiana, if there's a way to get there, without raising more questions." Silvia walked slowly, not wanting to catch up to her aunt or others who might overhear their conversation. "It's just that I don't want to tell anyone what we're doing or what we need or what we're looking for. All that information can't get out, until I know what I might find out about my ancestors." They walked along in silence as her Aunt Ida finished talking with other church goers and started toward the car.

"Come along, Silvia. You always dawdle. Move." Ida Strausburger spoke sharply as she limped along on an arthritic hip that wanted to sit on a pillowed chair. She could have brought a cushion to church, to pad the wooden pew. But, she enjoyed a certain amount of pain and discomfort that, to her mind, was proof of her martyrdom and sacrifice.

Silvia rolled her eyes and waited until Ida was out of ear shot. "I have more to lose than you do, Millie. I am part Shawnee. Your grandfather was just a kind man. I will receive the brunt of the teasing."

"I know. I know. But, I'll also have to explain how the Indians killed my distant grandmother's first husband. The settlers had come into Indian lands you know, not the other way around. We were the trespassers, even if the government had opened the territory to settlers."

Then her eyes brightened and a smile spread across her face. "I'll write a letter to the library in Union City and see if there's a book on the early settlers. I don't know much about the Brysons, except my grandfather, Isaac Newton Bryson, who was Daddy's father. And, what Daddy told me on the way back from getting ice cream." She smiled again, "Did you hear how my mother nearly popped her corset, when Daddy talked about James Bryson?"

"That was a surprise. I like your suggestion about writing a letter to the library. Now, that's a good idea." Then she stopped. "I won't be able to get a two-cent stamp from Aunt Ida. In your letter, could you ask about the Native Americans who lived in the area, especially the Shawnee tribe? Maybe they have a book or some information I could use."

"You mean your aunt won't give you two cents?"

"Not a single penny."

"We can do this . . . somehow. There has to be a way. We don't have much time." Millie pressed her hat up against her ears for warmth.

The pastor walked past them on his way home for Sunday dinner. "No, not much time until dinner," he joined in the conversation and then he hurried on.

Both girls laughed. "What must people think we're talking about?" Silvia joked.

Millie reached for the watch that hung around her neck and flipped it over to check the time. "He must really be hungry. It's not even noon yet."

"I thought that was a locket. It's a watch, too? Jake," Silvia laughed. "And it only reminds me of how much time is left before Indian day," she moaned.

"I was wondering if maybe we could get a ride into Union City on the milk truck." Millie snatched little Jerry Stringer's red stocking cap off his head as he ran past.

"Hey, give that back," he whined as he grabbed it from her.

Silvia dismissed the boy with a wave of her hand. "Millie, even if we could get a ride into town, wouldn't you still have to explain where you're going to your parents?"

"I know, I know. There has to be a way." She stopped before she got too close to her mother. "I'll start with the letter. Let's hope that works."

. . . . .

"You take that back, Herbert Schmidt!" Millie yelled and pushed him into the slushy snow near the school door.

It had been snowing every day for a full week since the basketball game. Each day there was a little more piled up on roads and fields. The ground was still not frozen far enough down to keep the puddles from freezing solid, so Herbert fell on his backside, and got his coat and pants dripping wet with icy water.

They both heard Miss Hollander jerk the large, heavy school room window up and shout with surprise. "Millie! Herbert! Both of you come in here right now!"

"Now you're in trouble, Miss Smarty," Herbert mocked as he tried to brush any remaining ice from his clothing.

"Well, I'd rather be smart and in trouble, than dumb like you, whether I'm in trouble or not." Millie turned up her nose, stomped the snow off her feet and went into the building. Herbert trailed behind her like a whipped, sopping wet puppy.

Their teacher waited for them in the hall outside the classroom. Her arms were folded sternly across her chest. "What on earth has gotten into you, Millie?"

"Herbert," she barked back. "He would not stop teasing and harassing me, about something I cannot help. So, I stopped him."

"Herbert . . ." Miss Hollander drew his name out in a deathblow of accusation. "What is this all about?"

"I don't know?" he said innocently.

"You do too, Herbert Schmidt! You most certainly do." Millie's eyes were flashing and her jaw was set in anger. "You called me an Indian-lover. There aren't even any Indians around here anymore." She knew that was a fib. Silvia was an Indian, but she hadn't even known it ten days before.

"So, are you saying, we are all supposed to be unkind to people who are different than we are? What limits would you put on your dislike?" Miss Hollander leaned her body toward him, like a deer with his antlers poised for attack.

"There isn't anyone around here different than us," he continued to protest. "I wouldn't have said it, if I really thought it was true."

"Herbert, that doesn't make any sense. I want you to go in and sit on the radiator until your pants dry. And, while you're there, you will write one-hundred times, 'People who are different are beautiful'."

"Yes, Miss Hollander," he dragged out in a prolonged whine. It had long been suspected that Herbert never did his homework. Now, he had to write more sentences than he had probably written all year long, right there in front of the teacher and the whole class.

"If you think I'm joking, I can discuss the assignment with your father. We'll see if he thinks it's funny."

"Yes, Ma'am," he moaned and walked into the classroom.

"Miss Hollander, I am sorry . . . but he —"

"I understand, Millie. Maybe I have put you and Silvia in a place that is not fair to either of you." She put her hand on Millie's shoulder and gave it a reassuring giggle.

"That's okay," Millie started and then added. "Actually, to tell the truth, I'm getting curious."

Her teacher threw her head back and laughed. "Why does that not surprise me?"

"Yes, Ma'am." Millie started into the classroom.

"Oh, a letter came here at the school for you. It had my name on it too, so it was placed in my box. Wait here. Mr. Schmidt doesn't need to hear your business." She retrieved the letter from the corner of her desk and took it back to the coat closet.

"Great! It must be from the library." Millie hung up her coat and turned as the precious letter was placed in her hand. "The only pieces of mail I get are birthday and Christmas cards from my grandparents." She slid her fingernail under the flap and pulled out a sheet of paper with a watermark right in the middle — Union City Library.

"Is it important?" Miss Hollander seemed excited for her.

"It is very important." She folded the paper and inhaled deeply. "Miss Hollander, I won't be able to give my outline speech today." She held the paper out for her to read.

"Thank you for your inquiry, Miss Bryson. We have many books in the library but, I'm sorry to say, we do not have the histories of the Ohio counties. Our library is small and we have only Indiana texts. As for the books on the Shawnee tribe, those are reference books and they cannot be checked out. However, you and your friend are welcome to come into the library and read the books in the reading room. Sincerely, Grace Miller, Head Librarian."

"I am sorry I've make your task more difficult than the others. You and Silvia are both good students. You each always hand your work in on time." She thought for a moment. "We won't possibly be able to hear all the students in one day, with all of our other work." She lowered her voice to a whisper as the other students began to come into the room. "We will plan to hear from you and Silvia on Monday next."

"Oh thank you," Millie sighed with relief.

"Miss Hollander!" Herbert shrieked. "My pants are on fire!"

"Herbert," she dropped her shoulders in resignation and started back into the classroom. There was smoke rising from the radiator beneath the boy's trousers. She screamed, "Get off that thing!"

Herbert hopped down and smacked at his smoking pants with both hands. Then, sheepishly, he pulled a small bundle of stick matches from his hip pocket, several of which had already ignited.

"Herbert Schmidt, I declare, you are either going to kill yourself, or do me in. The verdict is out on that." Miss Hollander took her last bouquet of mums from its vase, and threw the water on his backside. What might have already dried was re-soaked in the line of fire safety.

"Hey, Millie, I wondered what happened to you," Steven joked as he hurried to his seat before the bell rang. "Why is Herbert smoking?"

"Oh, you know Herbert. Anything he can do to get attention, is what he's going to do."

Steven shrugged in indifference. As he swung into his desk seat, he leaned forward and whispered, "You're going down, Bryson. Be prepared to be bested by the greatest orator of the school. I'm beating you today."

"Today, perhaps you will, Mr. Lawrence. But . . . just today."

8

The Library

"Millie, over here," Silvia whispered as the class began to leave the room at the end of the school day. She held something in her hand.

"What is it?"

Herbert jostled the girls and pushed them into the row of coats. "Always secrets with you two," he mocked.

"We tend to keep important, life-saving knowledge to ourselves. We wouldn't tell you if your hair was on fire," Millie shot back with a wave of her hand. "Oh, wait. It was your pants."

"Miss Hollandar," he called in a tattling tone.

"How old are you, five?" Silvia put her hand on her hip and spit out her disgust.

"I think you may have more sentences to write tomorrow," Miss Hollander said to Mr. Obnoxious. "What do you think, Mr. Schmidt?"

"I think I've written enough today, Ma'am. But, thank you for asking." He grabbed up his coat and hurried out the door.

Millie watched him leave, and then turned to Silvia in a hushed tone. "Okay, what do you have?"

Silvia opened her hand to reveal a set of car keys.

"Silvia," she gasped, "what have you done?"

"It is already Wednesday, and our presentations are due, maybe Friday if everyone talks fast. Or, at least on Monday, like Miss Hollander said. It's harvest time, Millie. The snow came early, and the crops have to be out of the field. Your parents can't take us to Greenville, and neither can Aunt Ida or Uncle Wilber. Aunt Ida is going to Richmond in my uncle's truck. She has to pick up a machinery part that he will need tomorrow. While she's there, she is going to attend a ladies meeting with some old school friends. Uncle Wilber will be busy in the fields. And, so will your parents, until late into the evening."

"But, Silvia . . . you are going to steal their car?" Millie whispered in fear. She dare not think what the Strausburgers would do if they were to find out. "What if someone sees us in Greenville and tells them?"

"Then, we'll say we got a ride into town."

"Maybe—"

"Millie . . . I'm going. Are you with me or not?"

"I'll have to go with you. You shouldn't do this alone."

"Get on the bus and go home as usual. Leave a note for your mom and dad. If they come in from the fields before we get home, they'll not wonder where you are."

"What am I supposed to lie to them about, Silvia? I'm not good at this." Millie was nervous. She had never deceived her parents before. At least, not anything big like this.

"Just tell them . . . you're with me." Silvia flipped the red scarf with the black stripe over her shoulder.

With that settled, Millie boarded the bus. If asked, Mr. Schmidt could say that he had dropped her off at the end of her lane as usual.

"What are you so skittish about?" Steven said when she sat down beside him. "Oh, I know. It's because I beat you today," he smirked.

"You can't beat someone if they haven't participated in the contest, Steven Lawrence. Miss Hollander got around to your speech today, and she'll come to mine tomorrow . . . or Friday . . . or Monday."

"I suppose that's a new kind of order. Is 'B' now at the end of the alphabet? Answer me that, Miss Bryson," Steven quizzed her. He was obviously getting a great deal of fun out of the situation.

"Yes, I guess," she said absentmindedly. Her focus was still on the car keys Silvia had held in her hand. This wasn't a game. Silvia could be in a lot of trouble if she were caught.

"What?" Steven sputtered and shook his head.

The day had been a stressful one, and the fields passed by the window in silence. Millie got up without speaking and got off the bus.

She hurried up the lane and was glad the snow had stopped earlier that day, around nine a.m. After Herbert sat in the slush puddle, it had thawed all day. It was almost an autumn day again, if it weren't for the clouds that had gathered. Could change happen so fast?

Out beyond the fence, the crops were nearly half down. Perhaps Daddy would have the harvest completed by Saturday. Inside, the back porch held the same chore list, tucked securely in the casement of the window. Millie grabbed it out, turned it over and scrawled, "Dear ones, I am spending the afternoon with Silvia. Our speeches will be due by the end of the week, and we need to do some more research. Not sure what time I'll be back. Don't worry. See you later. Millie." That would have to do. But, she knew her mother would worry if she came in and the house was empty. She would have to watch the time.

She hurried back out the door and closed it just in time to keep Fussbudget from darting in again. It was much warmer. Millie smiled at the cat and sympathized. "Don't get used to the kitchen, little girl. You know Mother wants you to stay outside."

Out on the road, Silvia waited with her aunt and uncle's Chevrolet purring in her hands. Millie looked the car and driver over, and wondered if either of them knew what they were getting into. She opened the door and jumped in.

"I didn't know you could drive," Millie said with amazement.

"I didn't either."

"Then how . . .?" Millie knew that she would never be able to sit behind the wheel. She didn't even pay any attention when her father or mother drove.

Bertha had simply driven round and round in the barnyard, until she felt confident enough to drive out of the lane and down the road. Millie had watched from the porch and then ran to catch up when her mother was ready for her maiden voyage.

She thought it best to not ask any questions that afternoon with Silvia. She might not have liked the answer.

"I watch Uncle Wilber all of the time, how to put the car in gear, what to watch for when you back up, how close to get to the cars beside you. I had to know how to drive. I've plotted my escape for two years," Silvia said quietly, seriously.

"Silvia . . . I am so sorry." She couldn't say more about how hard Silvia's live had been. She knew what she had seen with her own eyes. But, that afternoon, she had to make sure Silvia knew that she cared.

"It's only about ten miles to Greenville. There aren't very many stops on this road. It's not the breaks that bother me. It's starting the car again, that's the hardest." They both laughed.

The countryside moved past in slow motion. Silvia didn't drive very fast. It was easy to see how the early snow had caused the famers to work late into each evening, to save the crop they had worked so hard on. They had to get them out of the ground, fast.

· · · · ·

In Greenville, they slowly moved down Broadway toward the library. The store fronts were bright with fall colors on clothing, shoes, and all the displays that made the town inviting. For some reason, it felt warmer in town, happier. At least, Millie thought it did.

"It's just down a few blocks, and then behind the court house." Since she didn't have to watch out the front windshield as much as the driver did, Millie turned frequently to look for movement behind. She wanted to help Silvia, so she wouldn't have to change lanes without knowing what was behind her. Then, there it was. She had seen it before. The same truck that had followed them out of Indiana was back there again. Millie felt uncomfortable. "I'm beginning to think everyone is suspicious," she admitted.

"Why, what's wrong?"

"It feels like we're being followed."

"This is town. Of course there are others on the road."

"I guess you're right," Millie sighed, but still felt uneasy. She tried to shake it off by focusing on the assignment.

Their first stop was the library. There had to be something there to give them a clue to both of their ancestral pasts.

Silvia parked the car in a curb-facing parking spot out front. As they hopped out of the car, Millie turned and watched the street again.

"Wait," she grabbed Silvia's arm and pointed causally at the truck that approached from the west. Millie reached for her friend's coat and pulled her behind a tree in the front lawn of the library.

"What?"

Millie placed her finger to her lips and pointed to a store across the street. "Just pantomime, like we're talking about something, until he passes."

"Why? Who?" She whispered.

"Okay, he passed." She took Silvia by the arm and led her quickly into the library. "That same truck passed us again. He may not be following us, but he has been behind us at every turn. Call it whatever you want to." They hurried up the steps and into the strong walls that held the secrets of which the girls were searching.

"Good afternoon," Millie whispered to the librarian.

"Good afternoon, girls."

"I'm looking for a book about the history of Greenville," she said with all the confidence she could find. She knew she would draw attention to both of them if she appeared frightened or ill at ease. After all, they did have a stolen car parked at the curb.

"I'm here to help. Most of the children call me Miss Books, a little nickname. You're young ladies, but that will still work." She removed the glasses she had stored on the top of her head and swung them by the stem in a circle for a minute. Then she said, "*There is the History of Darke County Ohio, from its Earliest Settlement to the Present Time* by Frazer Wilson, Published in 1914. Let me show you." She led the way to the stacks, with Millie and Silvia close behind making silent victory signs to each other.

Miss Books pulled the volume from the stack and handed it to them. The girls scrambled over to one of the tables, threw their coats over the backs of chairs, spread the book out and went directly to the index of names in the back. Millie quickly ran her finger down the list, first the A's, and then . . . there it was, Bryson. She leafed through the pages.

"The Indian tribe had been divided about whether to let the settlers expand further west into Indian Territory, or to fight to keep them out." Millie looked up from the book. "That's interesting. I always thought that Indians fought about everything."

Miss Books smiled. "There are a lot of misperceptions about that time in our history. You read on. I'll be over at the desk if you need anything else."

"Okay, Miss Books, thank you." Millie began to study the history book again.

"Read it out loud. Maybe there's stuff in there for me, too."

"Okay, let's see," Millie began again. "It says the Shawnee Chief, Tecumseh, and his brother, the Prophet, convinced the rest of their scattered tribe to remain in what would be Darke County. They built a counsel house on land that, in 1919 when the book was written, was owned by James Bryson. His farm and several other farms are located where the village was. It was in Section nine, Township eleven."

"Great, the book gives a specific spot where the farm was. We could actually find it. Read on." Silvia got closer to the book as she leaned on the table.

"Let's see," Millie read some more. "Here. When the Prophet died, he was buried on a knoll by the counsel house where James Bryson's orchard stands." She looked up at Silvia, hoping to read her expression. "So, it's true."

"That is so jake*." Silvia threw her arms around Millie and jumped up and down, until she saw Miss Books wag her finger and insist on quiet.

Millie was relieved by Silvia's enthusiasm. She didn't seem to reject her, because of what her distant grandfather had done. She actually thought the whole idea was interesting. But then, Silvia had a lot more to lose. Millie's eyes grew big as she continued.

"Tecumseh and the Prophet had two completely different opinions about what the Shawnee people should do. The Prophet had learned of love from missionaries. He wanted their tribe to stop warring, attacking settlers and trying to drive them back." She paused and scanned the next few pages. "It's all here. We have our reports and our ammunition against Herbert Schmidt."

Silvia threw her arm around Millie's shoulder and jumped for joy, in pantomime, of course, so as not to disturb the others. "Yes, but everyone remembers the uncivilized Tecumseh, not his brother who preached love and belief in God. Now, we can tell them all!" Her eyes shone with joy and relief. "That is amazing. The Shawnee Indians were not all savages. There were good people among them . . . and those are my ancestors, just like James is your ancestor." She bounced with excitement as she threw her arm around Millie again. "Let's go find the farm. We can describe the area first hand, for our reports."

"Did you find what you need?" The soft spoken librarian asked. It was evident how happy the girls looked. "Can I help you with anything else?"

"Well, we know where the parcel of land is, but we don't' know where the location is. In other words, I see where my great-great-grandpa lived, but I don't know how to get there."

"Oh, you girls need the plat maps. They're right over here." The librarian silently floated across the room, past the fireplace, and into another room of the library. No matter how hard she tried, Millie couldn't seem to keep her shoes as silent on the hardwood floors as Miss Books did.

"They're here in the library? That's great," Millie bubbled as she and Silvia hurried behind her. "We thought we'd have to go over to the Court House for that information."

"Let's see." Miss Books ran her finger across the huge shelved volumes until she came to the binding label that corresponded to the proper date. "Here it is." She withdrew a large book from the shelf and spread it open on the library table.

The two girls huddled over the map and searched each sector. "Let's see . . . Section nine of Greenville Township." Then she stopped, with her finger on the lower left quarter. "Silvia, there . . . there's his name, James Bryson."

They poured over the map and looked for other land marks they could recognize. Nothing on the map looked familiar to them. "Miss Books, now I need to know how to recognize it."

"I know the area pretty well. Let's get the current map of the county and see." The helpful librarian scanned the map and then stopped. "Okay . . . the farm is bounded by the Hollansburg-Arcanum Road, Butler Township Road, Hursch Road and Emerick Road."

The girls hugged and jumped for joy. "Thank you, thank you, thank you," Millie chattered as she got out a pencil and paper to write down the adjacent roads.

"Miss Books," Silvia had been excited about what they had found. Now, she had another question. "What about the Shawnee Indians?" She held her breath and wrinkled her nose. "Is there more on them?"

"You'll find information about the early Indians on the pages just before the section about James Bryson in that first history book you were reading. A history certainly is not complete without recognizing the first people who settled here." She smiled at each of them. "I'm glad I could help."

"Maybe we didn't go back far enough to get the whole story." Silvia grabbed Millie's arm.

The girls hurried back into the first room where the book still remained on the table. Silvia fanned through the pages of the History of Darke County that preceded the Bryson connection. She scanned down the page and then stopped. "This is just what I need!" She was so excited her feet could not keep from dancing as she bent over the table.

"They built a village they called Prophetstown," she continued, "a counsel house and some small homes. Tecumseh was mad. He devised a plan to discredit the Prophet."

Millie's eyes danced with excitement. "Silvia, just like everybody else. Some Shawnee were good people and some, not so good. The Prophet taught Christian love and responsible living. You can be very proud of him."

"There's someone else . . ." Silvia whispered.

"Who? Here in Greenville?"

"I think he may be near James Bryson's farm. I hope I remember right." She started to continue and then added, "We'll talk as we go. We don't want to be any later getting home than absolutely necessary."

The girls grabbed their coats and threw them on as they darted from the library. Out on the road, they jumped into the Aunt Ida's Chevrolet. Silvia stopped, frozen behind the wheel.

"What's wrong?" Millie questioned with excitement.

"I've only started this thing once, about an hour ago." She stared at the dashboard and steering wheel. "At least, I didn't have to parallel park. But, I'm . . . well, I'll have to back out of here, which may be almost as bad. Backing up involves the clutch."

"Let's see . . . it's not that hard." She looked at Millie and held her breath. Neither said another word. Silvia checked over her left shoulder, then her right. She pressed in the clutch pedal with her left foot and pushed on the starter with her right. Then, she shifted it into reverse with her right hand on the gear shift, pressed her foot on the accelerator and let up on the clutch. She tried to feel for the balance, the friction point . . . sputter . . . sputter . . . stall.

"You can do it, Silvia," Millie encouraged.

Clutch . . . gas . . . friction point . . . spit . . . stall. "There has to be a way," Silvia whispered, frustrated but determined.

"I'll jump out and push you back," Millie suggested.

"Okay . . . wait. The car is angled down toward the curb. You would be pushing it up hill. I think not, Millie."

"Hey Girlie – you gonna move that car?" a familiar voice growled from behind them.

"Don't turn around, Millie!" Silvia whispered hoarsely. "Don't even look back. It's Herbert Schmidt." They slid down in their seats and hid, as if no one would notice their strange behavior.

Another driver, in a farm truck, pulled up behind Herbert and revved his engine. Schmidt didn't move. The dark figure with a straw farm hat pulled low over his eyes, moved up closer to Herbert's bumper. He gunned the engine again and pushed the Schmidt truck along the street, even with the brakes pushed to the floor.

Herbert moved slowly past the Chevrolet, whether he wanted to or not, then coasted a few spaces after the truck behind him stopped pushing.

"We can't be seen in Aunt Ida's car," Silvia reminded her. The girls slipped out of the car on the opposite side from where Herbert landed, crouched in front of two cars, and then stepped from the street onto the sidewalk.

"Over here," Millie coaxed as she slithered over to a public bench that faced the library, and away from the street. "If we act very casual, maybe he'll go on home." They sat down and started a whispered, very neutral conversation.

"It is a beautiful afternoon, isn't it?" Silvia began.

"The snow has stopped and it's a little warmer," Millie replied. "I hate to see the pretty leaves fall, all the color and fire. The wind last evening and heavy rain dropped most of them that had lingered."

"Boo!" A voice announced behind them. Both girls were startled. "What are you two whispering about?" Herbert oozed as he snuck up behind them. "What are you doin' in Greenville?"

"Mother needed some dark blue thread and we had a ride into town, so we came to pick it up."

"Where is it?"

"Where's what?"

"The thread," he blurted out rudely.

"Oh . . . we didn't buy it yet," Millie answered confidently.

"Who brought you into town? You said you had a ride."

"It's none of your business. I won't give you their name. If you talk to them, they might find out you are as annoying as we think you are," she asserted with her chin held high.

"Maybe Indian-lovers ain't allowed in the stores. Did you think about that?"

"Fools aren't allowed," Millie announced with authority. "But, proper people are welcome anywhere."

With that, the girls turned their backs on Herbert, got up from the bench and walked swiftly along Sycamore Street to the corner, up to Fifth Street, then onto Broadway.

9

The Straw Hat

The girls made their way through the double doors of the Palace Department Store. Fall colors of gold, umber and brilliant red were everywhere. Millie wanted to drink in all the beauty around her that stimulated her desire to stop and browse. But, she didn't. If she didn't get home before her mother came in, she would have too much explaining to do.

Midway back through the store, past the shoes and handbags, the elevator was on the right. They fixed their eyes on the doors and headed that way.

"There he is again," Millie whispered when she saw a young man in a straw farm hat. "What is he doing in here?"

"It's a department store. Maybe he's here to buy a new hat," Silvia chuckled.

"Look at this." Millie picked up a pair of white kid gloves and tried on the right one.

"I thought we were in a hurry."

"We are," she smiled and laughed as she removed the glove.

"Then, what are you doing?"

"Stalling," Millie whispered and looked in the direction of the elevator. "I'm waiting for Mr. Hat to leave. He makes me feel uncomfortable. I think he's following us."

"Don't be silly. Maybe he's doing his Christmas shopping early."

They looked again, but the fellow was gone, so they hurried over to the lift. As they pushed the button and stepped onto the elevator, hat-man darted around the corner from behind a display of winter coats, and slipped onto the elevator car*. Millie's body tensed. Her breathing increased and she felt very uneasy.

Hat-man stepped close beside Silvia and ran his fingers over the hand-woven wool strip around her neck. "I like your scarf."

"Thank you," she said but didn't turn around. "It was my father's. Today is the day I need to wear it."

"I have to get out of here," Millie gasped as she closed her eyes in the tiny space.

"Get out? We're between floors. We'll be there in a matter of seconds," Silvia soothed.

When the doors opened, Millie pushed her way off the elevator box, grabbed hold of a display table and inhaled deeply. She glanced back at the straw hat man and her face was stiff with fear. Their eyes met.

"I'm sorry," the man said. He looked disappointed, not dangerous. He pushed the button on the elevator panel again and the door closed with him inside.

"What's wrong with you?" Silvia pulled on Millie's arm and waited for an answer.

"That man frightens me," was all she could say.

"Why? Do you know him?"

"No." She checked back to make sure he wasn't behind them anymore. "But Silvia, he was following us. If he didn't want me to be afraid of him, he shouldn't have been behind us everywhere we went." She removed her coat and threw it over her arm. She had to take control of herself and chose to focus on things around her.

Yard goods and fabric bolts were everywhere, on shelves behind the long counter and on display tables in the middle of the room. Whatever the imagination could dream up to sew on a treadle sewing machine, danced as possibilities from the colors and textures in front of them. The darker colors of winter were displayed on wide tables, with the colors of autumn scattered through them for excitement.

"Hi Millie," the clerk smiled at the girls as they browsed through the fabrics and sundry* items. "What do you need today?"

"Mother needs a spool of dark blue thread to finish the hem to the dress she made. She bought the fabric in here," Millie said as she looked around the tables and shelves of bolted fabrics.

"I believe she bought her yardage from this bolt." The clerk pulled some piece-goods from the shelf behind her.

"Yes Ma'am. I'm sure that's it. I was with her. She took it from that spot." Millie went to the display of threads, removed two spools from the case and took them to the clerk.

"We'll have to try to move the car again," Silvia muttered in defeat as Millie made her decision on the thread.

"Aren't automobiles a nuisance, dear?" The clerk agreed. "Just put it in gear, find your friction point with your clutch and gas, and then sloooowly increase the gas, keeping the clutch on that sweet spot. You'll be fine." She took the thread, rang up the purchase and then asked Silvia, "How long have you been driving?"

"It seems like minutes, when I have to back out." She smiled a sweet smile.

"Thanks," they chimed in together, as the clerk handed Millie the bag.

Millie placed the purchase in her coat pocket and then slipped her arms in the sleeves. Soon, they were back down on the elevator, through the first floor and outside. They crossed the street, walked up a block and got into the car – then the rehearsed – clutch, put in gear, turn on engine, balance the gas and clutch.

"Do you need some help?" The dark fellow in the straw hat asked as he leaned on the driver's side window.

"I think I have it," Silvia said as she blushed.

"We'd better go," Millie coaxed, uneasy about the ever-present, but unknown helper. "You think he's not stalking us now?"

"Thanks again," Silvia answered, held her breath and slowly backed out. She finally exhaled. At the corner, they turned and followed Route 127 out into farm country.

Millie turned around and watched the road behind them for several miles. She would have recognized the man's truck by then. It wasn't there. They were on their way to Section 9, Township 11.

10

The Quest

"It is so beautiful out here," Millie sighed as she watched the passing country through the Chevrolet side-window.

It was much like the drive to Randolph County, Indiana. Farm houses dotted the land, with adjacent barns and other out-buildings. Smoke rose from chimneys connected to fireplaces and coal furnaces. When the girls actually turned onto the northern boundary of the section, the Hollansburg-Arcanum Road, then turned left onto Butler Township Road, there seemed to be something even more exciting about the area. At least to Millie's mind it was. Perhaps it was just the heart of a Bryson child returning home to the first recorded evidence of her family's settlement in Darke County.

"James was my great-great grandfather. The County History said that he bought his farm in 1817. His son, Joseph, lived on the place until he died in 1909. Joseph had never married. We found his last will and testament, which simply stated, after all expenses and special legacies to family members were paid, the real estate would be divided among all his nephews and heirs. I don't know who lives there now, family or strangers."

"We can't just walk up to the front door," Silvia said as she slowed at the end of the lane.

"There aren't any lights on." Millie studied the house and scanned every inch, from the front door, up on the roof to the lightning rods, and down the sides.

"What are we going to do?' Silvia puzzled as she watched Millie's face set in determination. "Break in?"

"Silvia! Of course not. But . . . I would like to walk around in the yard and barn. I don't think anyone would care about that."

The two story frame house stood back from the road on a little knoll that overlooked an apple orchard. "I wonder what it looked like when James and Rachael lived here. My mother's family farm house had been a log cabin. They cooked their meals over the fireplace. As the family grew, they needed more space and they built the house around the cabin. I imagine Daddy's family could have done the same."

"The orchard? Don't you remember? The Prophet was buried in what became James Bryson's orchard. It is right here, Millie." Silvia pointed out the obvious grove of apple trees.

The gravel crunched beneath their tires as they pulled close to the edge of the road and Silvia parked the car. The girls slowly got out and continued to study the house to see if there was any movement. A red cardinal watched from the top of a tree that had already donated its fruit to the family who lived on the farm. That was the only thing that moved.

Finally, Millie had to do something. She couldn't just stand in the middle of the lane. She crouched a little and darted up behind one of the tree trunks in the orchard and gave exaggerated motions for her friend to follow.

Silvia obediently moved toward the clump of apple trees, but slower, and with far less enthusiasm. "Millie, are you slumped over because you think they won't see you behind a small fruit tree?"

"I feel like I'm trespassing, so I guess I'm trying to hide."

"You . . . we . . . *are* trespassing, silly."

Sylvia stomped on the ground beneath the trees, and brushed the fallen leaves back with the toe of her shoe. "Just think. The Prophet is right beneath our feet."

"It's amazing," Millie whispered. "I don't see anyone around the place." She looked toward the white frame house and the barnyard. It was all trimmed and polished. Whitewashed rocks lining the drive and out to the tall red barn. "Come on, let's go."

The girls walked past a chicken yard, complete with a red building, with a little ramp up to the chicken coop door. The rooster crowed and strutted about; several chickens fluttered and flapped their wings, running into each other behind him.

The barn was a proud structure of tall planks under a roof of black shingles. Inside, the scent of animals was mixed with the rich aroma of harness leather. It really was no different than any other barn Millie had been in, but it felt like home. Birds flew from the rafters and out the open windows that were high in the barn.

"Just think, Sylvia, this is where Grandpa James had worked every day of his life." She took a pencil and a pad of paper from her pocket, and began to sketch the interior of the barn. When she walked back out into the barnyard, she captured the house, the orchard and the barn in a quick sketch of the whole layout.

While Millie was occupied, Silvia walked around the barnyard and orchard. Slowly, she put out her hand and touched the bark of the trees, as if the life in the soil below could reach her palm. Then she stopped. The late afternoon wind had stirred the fallen leaves and carried their scent in the air. A campfire was burning someplace. Not a fireplace, an open, outside fire. Her head suddenly shot up, like a doe that had sniffed the air and discovered a mystery.

"Come on," she whispered, as she faced into the wind. "This way."

"Where are we going?" Millie asked as she walked down the lane with her toward the woods.

In the field to the left, Holstein cows* grazed in the cold sunshine and a bull could be seen snorting from a distance. The huge bull followed the girls with his eyes, but stayed where he was. Millie smelled the burning wood too. Its smoke rose in a fine thread above the trees in a clearing in the woods.

When the girls got to the tree line, they hung back, just barely inside the woods, and watched with wide eyes. There in a small clearing, was a teepee covered in deer hide, with its east-facing flap door open. Smoke rose up through the opening created at the top of the structure, where the lodgepole pines met the sky. The light inside was dim from a distance, but they could see a small bonfire, bordered in rocks in the middle of the room. An old man with long gray hair, holding a white bowled pipe with a long-stem and glowing embers, was inside.

"Old Grandfather?" Silvia whispered.

"He's your Grandfather?"

"Yes, but I don't remember if I have ever met him. He is my great-grandfather and he is very old. He lives mostly in silence and prays to the Great Spirit above."

"Are we going in?" Millie asked as she watched Silvia plant her feet firmly on the edge of the woods.

"No," she gasped. "He spends his days in prayer."

"Well, I didn't come all this way to hide among the trees." And with that, Millie stepped into the clearing.

"Millie! No!" she hissed from the clearing's edge.

Millie turned, pursed her mouth, stomped her foot, and walked directly toward the open flap of the teepee. She didn't pause a second. Bending low, she stuck her head inside. There were no other openings in the hide, so Millie had to adjust her eyes to the dimmer light as she looked around.

"Come in, Little Bryson," the old one said. He did not stand up. With his pipe in his hand, he slowly blew circles of smoke in the air around him.

"How did you know my name?" she gulped with amazement.

"You do not live on this farm. The only ones who have come into my teepee have been my kinfolk, the Shawnee, and the Brysons who used to live here." He smiled and puffed on his pipe. "And the necklace you wear belonged to Rachel Bryson."

"Yes, it did. She was my great-great grandmother." She touched her locket-watch and felt a connection with her distant past. "Just a minute, Sir." She smiled graciously and turned to Silvia, who still stood half-way behind a tree. "It is okay, Silvia," she shouted as she waved a join-me gesture in her direction.

"Little Owl is with you," he stated with certainty. "I see her in the shadows of the trees."

"Little Owl?"

A shadow crossed the floor inside the opening, as Silvia stuck her head into the round space. She smiled but said nothing.

"Little Owl," the old one pronounced. "Come all the way into my space, or back yourself out. It is very uncomfortable to be bent over, neither in nor out. You cannot remain *nowhere*. You must decide."

"Old Grandfather," she said, stopped, and then ventured all the way into the room.

"Sit," he said with a wave of his hand as he pointed to mats on the floor. "Now, tell me, what do you want to know?"

"You mean you don't know? I mean, since you know who we are." Millie questioned, unsure of the old one's wisdom.

"I recognized you by your locket and Little Owl is wearing her father's scarf. I met when she was very small."

"I do think I remember you, Old Grandfather," Silvia admitted.

"I may know what you want to know," he answered wisely, as he puffed on his pipe. "But, if you cannot put your question into words, you do not know what you want to know."

The room was warm and comfortable; fur pelts were scattered on the floor to sit on. Meat sizzled on the fire. It looked like a rabbit to Millie. The girls sat down on the soft covering and ran their fingers through the furs.

"Sir," Millie began. She was uncertain of the proper etiquette when conversing with an old Indian chief. "I must write about my distant grandfather's friendship with the Indians who had built their counsel building, and set their fire right here on what would become his farm. But, the connection didn't stop when the farm house was built and the family moved in. The history book said that his wife Rachel, my distant grandmother, was working in her kitchen one day, when she saw a band of Indians in her yard performing some ritual. They might have come often."

"Prophetstown was here." Old Grandfather spread his arms to show it covered a lot of land. "It extended up into the sections to the north. Our people came here often to pay our respects to our ancestors, to Tecumseh and his brothers Blue Jacket and the Prophet. Then, when your grandfather built his home on the knoll, he gave us permission to come and pay tribute to the Chiefs of old. I came as a child, too. Now, only I sit in the teepee of my ancestors and think of them. No one disturbs me . . . except, of course," he smiled broadly, "you two."

Millie looked around at the furs on the floor and the pottery jars that were placed near the side of the teepee. "The history books were confusing about where Blue Jacket and Tecumseh were buried, but it said the Prophet is here."

"The chiefs are where they are. But, yes, the Prophet drinks from the cider of your grandfather's orchard." He poked at the embers of the fire and tossed two more logs on their sparks. Then he turned the sizzling rabbit. The aroma filled the room and tormented those with hungry stomachs.

"But, Sir . . ."

"Old Grandfather they call me."

"Old Grandfather, when I write in my report that he is not only buried here, but that James and Rachel welcomed his people, they will call me an Indian-lover."

"Are you not one?" he asked, not with an accusing tone, but a knowing heart.

"I love Silvia, and she's Shawnee, and . . . I'm growing very fond of you."

"Those words, *Indian-lover*, bring up old pains from a long ago generation," he whispered. "The smoke from distant fires can still sting the eyes."

Millie thought about those words and nodded. A long ago injury can still hurt.

"But, we no longer have to experience that pain, if we choose not to." Old Grandfather stoked the fire and watched the sparks rise. "Young Bryson, if you love one and all, then you are an Indian-lover and . . . a people-lover. The truth cannot hurt you. With truth on your side, you cannot be shamed. When shame is thrown at your feet, you have to pick it up in order to feel bad about it."

"Thank you, Grandfather," Millie said as she watched the old one blow more smoke rings up the chimney hole.

"I hurt too, Old Grandfather." Silvia lowered her eyes and spoke softly. "I need to know about the Prophet. Some hate the Shawnee. They call the Indians, *savages*. They tease and taunt and call them names. They don't even know I'm one of them. My assignment, for the Indian paper, is to write about the Prophet. Miss Hollander said she knows that I'm Shawnee. I remember my father taking me to meet you, when I was very little. Daddy died in the war, then Mother died too, and Aunt Ida wouldn't tell me anything."

"Yes, your father was one-half Shawnee. He became a doctor, then, he had to go to the war. There were many men hurt in the fighting. The hospital was under attack, and your father died trying to save some of the patients. You can be very proud of that Shawnee."

"Thank you, Old Grandfather." Silvia's expression relaxed and she seemed relieved. "And now, I have to ask you to heal the name of the Prophet. The county history book said that the

Prophet was good. He wanted his people to find peace. Tell me about him, Grandfather."

"The Prophet learned love and peace from missionaries who came into the village a very long time ago. The Prophet preached to the people and they believed him." The old chief talked for a long time in the shelter of his teepee. The girls' faces glowed with the thrill of new understanding, and love for a people they had not known.

"But, Old Grandfather, I need to know what to say to those haters, like Herbert Schmidt."

"Little Mouse?" Old Grandfather laughed.

"Little Mouse?" Millie gasped. "He does seem like an annoying, disease carrying rodent, not even important enough to be a rat. How do you know him?"

"We know all of our tribesmen," the Old One answered, as he drew a picture of a mouse with his finger on the floor.

"Tribesmen?"

"Every answer is a question, Little Bryson."

"Then," Silvia asked slowly as reality soaked in, "Herbert is Shawnee?"

"One-half," he said with a smile.

"Yeah!" Both girls cheered. "Now we can keep him quiet. If he says one word, if he teases or calls us names, we can put him in his place."

"Then you are no different than the mouse. If it is not a bad thing to be Shawnee, then no one can accuse you of being one. You would wear the name with pride."

"But, Grandfather," Millie protested, "he has to know that we know. Where's the fun in having power over him, if he doesn't know it?"

"It is enough that you know. You can face him with the knowledge of who he is. It will give you strength and peace, knowing that you could destroy him, but choose to be at peace, just like the Prophet taught. Will you choose the peace the Prophet preached about, the peace of the Great Spirit, or will you continue the war Tecumseh waged? The answer to that question will determine if you are a savage or one of the peaceful people."

11

Back in Time

"Boy, we're just plain lucky," Silvia marveled as they pulled into Millie's farm lane. The sun was just beginning to slip behind the barn and cast long shadows across the yard. Even though the day was nearly spent, the tractor had not returned to the barn and the house was dark.

Millie quickly opened the car door and felt the wind kick up her skirt. "Brrr," she moaned. "I won't know if you get home okay until tomorrow at school. Be careful."

"I will . . . and, Millie thanks for going with me. I couldn't have done it alone." She had a puzzled look on her face and then added. "There are still a few questions I wish I had asked Old Grandfather."

Millie rested her hand on the car door and leaned inside. "Meet me near the cloak room tomorrow morning. I have to hear if your aunt knew that her car was missing."

"Okay." Silvia put the car in reverse, found the friction point between the clutch and the gas with ease, and backed out of the driveway.

Millie hurried into the house, hung her coat on the back porch rack, and dashed into the house. She retrieved the note she had left for her mother and flipped it over.

3.   Do your homework

Well, that one was easy. She had worked on the Indian assignment all afternoon.

2. We'll have leftover chicken and dumplings. The crock is cooling in the milk house. Put them on and we'll hope to be in by 6 p.m.

She picked up the watch that hung upside down on her bodice*, and checked the time. It was 5:30. There was enough time. She grabbed her coat, threw it around her shoulders, and went back outside to the little stone building that sat near the outdoor pitcher pump. It was dark in the milk house, but she could feel her way around. There were no milk cans at that time of day, because the milking was done in the early morning, and the milk man would have picked up the cans by 9 a.m. There was still enough light to see the crock, right where her mother said it would be. She reached for it cautiously, since mice had a way of finding a warmer spot once the corn in the fields started coming down. Millie hated mice.

With the crock in her hands, she turned to leave the small, cold room when she saw it. There, along the wall, just at the door, was the little varmint.

"Get out of here, Little Mousey Herbert." With that pronouncement, she slammed the door closed.

Back inside, she quickly began to prepare supper. With a hot pad in one hand, she opened the door to the firebox and checked the flame in the stove. Then she grabbed out a kettle and spooned the dumplings into the pot. It had started to steam and send yummy perfume into the room by the time her parents came into the house, tired and hungry.

"Millie, it smells wonderful," Bertha swooned as she sank down onto a chair.

"It sure does . . . but you could be boiling my old boots, and that would have smelled great too. I am so hungry." Daddy walked over to the sink. He picked up a basin, pumped water into it from the pitcher pump and then poured in some hot water from the teakettle. "Come Bertha, we'll wash our hands together, so neither of us can complain about dirty water."

"Why, Daddy, what a nice thing to say," she sounded surprised. Millie guessed she was more amazed by the number of words he used than the gesture.

With their hands clean, they set about putting the food on the table. Millie poured the coffee she had started after she had put the dumplings on to cook. She poured herself a cup as well. She didn't care much for milk, even though the icebox kept it nice and cold. Mother said grace, and then each picked up their fork and moved with the precision of a choreographed dance – dumpling, bread, beans – dumpling, bread, beans.

"You work so hard, both of you do." Millie started her questioning with praise, then questions. "Daddy, you read for the law exam. Why didn't you ever practice law? It might have been easier than farming."

"Maybe. But, I love the land. I think I breathe dirt. This is where I want to be."

"But, you said you had an uncle who was a common pleas* judge."

"Yes, old Uncle Joseph. But, he finally went back to farming, because that was his first love. Now, let's have no more talk of that nonsense. I'm hungry." With that, he dug into his supper, and the discussion was over.

Millie changed the subject. "Did anyone stop by the farm this afternoon?" She ventured a question.

"We were in the field all day. I packed us a lunch. You were here in the house," her mother stopped and looked up from her plate.

"Well, that's true. I checked in at home, and then left you a note. Silvia and I worked all afternoon on our Indian projects." She studied her napkin very intently, so as not to give away her anxiety.

"Oh good. But, I didn't see anyone around." Then she added, "Did you find what you need for your paper and talk?"

"Yes, we found a lot."

"That's good." Bertha covered her mouth in a yawn. "We're all tired. Maybe we can go to bed early. I know I can sleep. Harvest is going good. The yield looks great. Not a worry in the world."

"Not a worry," Millie agreed and remembered Old Grandfather.

Smoke from distant fires can sting the eyes. But, the truth cannot hurt you.

12

Gone

"Have you seen Silvia?" Millie asked Steven the next morning. She checked the classroom cloak area, and then her own time piece. Miss Hollander would sit at her desk in a few minutes, and she was to meet Silvia before school started.

She went to the window and looked out into the school yard. It looked like all the busses were in, and no one was on the road. She jumped with a start when the bell sounded. Silvia was late.

It was Thursday. Her speech would be due today or tomorrow. She couldn't think. She couldn't focus. Where was Silvia? Did Aunt Ida have her arrested for taking the car?

The morning ticked along. Sarah was up in front of the class talking about something. Millie had no idea what. Her mind was not in the classroom. It wasn't really anywhere. She was worried. Silvia was still not in school and it was 10:15.

"Excuse me, Miss Hollander," the principal apologized as he entered. "I have to ask Millie Bryson to step into my office for a few minutes."

Millie looked around to see if anyone else had noticed she was leaving. How silly was that? Of course everyone could see her being paraded out of the classroom. Steven touched her arm as she walked past him to the back of the row, then around to the left. The door was located on the back side corner of the room. She felt like she had been placed in a police line-up.

Millie followed Mr. Allen down the hall to his office. "What's the problem?" she asked nervously when he asked her to sit down opposite his desk.

"It's about Silvia Wagoner." He paused as another man came in. "Do you know Sheriff Cooper, Millie?"

"Yes, Sir. He and his Mrs. Go to our church." She looked from the Sheriff to Mr. Allen. Although she didn't know what she was doing in there, she could tell by their expressions, it was serious.

"Millie," the sheriff sat down beside her. "Silvia is missing. Her aunt said she had gone into her room this morning when she didn't hear her get up to do the milking, and she wasn't anywhere around the place. Her Uncle Wilber even went out into the woods. Ida said she was a friend of yours, that she had gone for ice cream with you and your folks and Sarah Dunleavy, the other evening. Ida said you are a good friend she trusts with her niece."

Millie shuddered as she thought about those words — she trusted me. "When did she turn up missing?"

"Ida said she had come home late in the evening yesterday, after being in Richmond. Wilber was in the fields all day, like all the other farmers. They said Silvia was in the sitting room at the oak table, doing school work. Ida said, 'Are ya getting that report on the Indians done?'

"The girl said, 'Yes, I am. What if I found some really interesting stuff? Maybe I had only suspected it in the past, but found out it was true? Would that be okay?'

"'What on earth are you talking about, Girl?' Ida had asked her.

"Then she says, 'Why don't you ever talk about my father?' And Ida said, I just asked her, 'What are you thinking about him for?' So, then she said, 'I heard something today.' Then Ida said that Silvia told her she had talked to someone called, Old Grandfather." Copper shook his head. "Do you know what she may have been talking about?"

What could Millie say? It sounded like no one knew Silvia had taken the car. It didn't seem fair to get her into trouble for something no one knew anything about.

"Silvia and I got a ride into Greenville to go to the library. We had to look up some information for a paper that would be due tomorrow."

"Did she say anything about an Old Grandfather?" The Sheriff asked.

"She wanted to talk to her grandfather. We got home before sundown."

The conversation turned from the grandfather to the important time line around her disappearance. "So you were both in before night fall?"

"I got out of the car first. Silvia had agreed to meet me before school this morning. You just told me that her Aunt Ida told you, Silvia was doing her homework when they came in."

"Yes, you're right." He turned to Principal Allen. "I would like the school's help."

"Sure, anything," he agreed.

"I would like for you to dismiss the eighth graders. They all know Silvia, and would recognize her. I could use them for a search party," he said.

"That would be great!" Principal Allen jumped up from his desk. "Come on," he said, as they hurried back down the hall with Millie close behind. She kept up a running argument with herself, inside her mind, as she followed.

Ida and Wilber saw her at home, after she let me off. Maybe I should have told them. Our drive into Greenville might be important. But, how could it be? The car is at the farm. Why pile on grand theft auto to her other crimes? They might even charge me for going along with her.

Inside the classroom, Sarah had finished her talk, and Polly had just been called on. "I'm sorry to interrupt again," Mr.

Allen announced. "I want you to give your full attention to Sheriff Cooper."

There were a lot of whispers and pokes. Silly nonsense like, "They finally tracked you down," buzzed around the room. But, by the time the sheriff walked to the head of the class, the only sound that was heard was the squeaking of Cooper's leather shoes on the highly polished, old hardwood floor boards.

"Thank you for allowing me to interrupt your class," he began. When he unbuttoned his jacket and sat down on the edge of the desk, Millie knew he was ready to get serious. "One of your classmates, Silvia Wagoner, has gone missing. Her aunt went to check on her early this morning, and she wasn't anywhere."

"Did you check their car?" Herbert asked loudly. "I think I saw her driving in Greenville yesterday."

"Silvia is only fourteen. I realize there is no age limit, but she doesn't seem old enough to drive," Miss Hollander offered what she believed to be the facts. "I have never seen her in the driver's seat of a car before."

"The Chevrolet is still parked at the farm," Sheriff Cooper stated.

"Well, she's one of those Indian lovers," Little Mouse jumped in again. "Maybe you'll find her on the reservation."

"There are no reservations in this area," Cooper added impatiently. Then he said quickly, before the mouse could stick his whiskers in again, "I'm here to ask all of you to help form a search party. Are any of you willing?"

Every hand in the class shot up. Words like, "You can count on me, Sheriff," were echoed all over the room.

Maybe you can track her, Herbert, just like any other Indian, Millie thought, but she didn't say it out loud.

"I've arranged for a school bus to be outside, to take us to Strausburgers' farm. We'll begin there, and fan out. You absolutely must be careful of the crops that are still standing in the fields. That's cash money out there. Don't step on any plants."

Everyone snatched up their coats and caps and hurried out to the bus. Miss Hollander was the last to board.

"Everyone take your seats quickly. Time may be important. We don't know what happened, but we do know she is missing."

The bus was surprisingly silent. Not even Herbert, the mouse, had anything to say. The roads were especially pitted from the heavy traffic of harvest tractors. The students bounced along, holding onto the back of the seat in front of them, to keep from landing in the aisle.

"We are here at the Strausburgers' farm," Miss Hollander announced. "Silvia's aunt and uncle are very upset, so let them talk to you, rather than you asking them a lot of questions. We will fan out from their house." She stood up and motioned for everyone to follow her. They all piled off the bus and waited politely for the Strausburgers to come out onto the porch.

"Thank you so much for your help," Wilber began. "We are very worried." His face was drawn, and concern etched deep lines in his forehead.

"I don't know where to begin," Ida stammered. "Silvia was here last evening. I was so tired, I went on to bed, and she was still up working on homework." Her face was strained and her eyes looked red from crying. "Silvia is very good about trimming the lamp before going to bed." Then her voice trailed off into sadness.

Millie could not believe Ida's display of emotions. She was obviously shaken and very upset. About what? Ida Strausburger had nothing good to say about Silvia just a few days past. Now, here she was, acting like a real person.

Sheriff Cooper stepped up onto the porch and spoke quietly to Ida and Wilber. Then he turned to the class. "I want you to look around the barnyard and all over the farm. You must stay in a straight line. If some of you get ahead of the others, you will walk all over any clues that might be found on the place."

The students did as they were told, and created a walking front, like in the game Red Rover. They wanted no clue to break through their line. Speaking only in whispers, they moved across the barnyard. The seriousness of the task had finally reached them, as they kept their eyes to the ground, looking for any scrap of evidence.

"I don't know what to look for," Steven whispered, as he fixed his eyes on the barnyard.

"Just anything that looks out of place, anything that isn't gravel, grain, or chicken hooey," Millie spoke plainly. She scanned the few inches right in front of her, all across the barn yard, not in the direction of the garage and the Chevrolet, but toward the barn. They had moved about forty feet, when she stooped and picked up a charm from a bracelet. "Silvia had this bracelet on yesterday when we . . ."

"When you what? Where did you two go?" Steven asked as he waved Sheriff Cooper over to them.

"We went into Greenville to go to the library," she said and offered no more.

"How?" But, his question was interrupted.

"Did you find something?" the Sheriff asked as he came over, in response to their urging.

"A charm," Millie offered as she handed it to him. "Silvia's mother had gone to the 1918 Chicago World's Fair and bought a charm bracelet. This is from that bracelet. When her mother died, her Aunt Ida reluctantly gave it to Silvia. She had it on yesterday. I saw it."

"That's great observation, Millie. So . . ." he looked from the house to the barn, "she came out this way."

Others moved past them in the huge people-wave that flowed across the property. Herbert Schmidt looked like he had found his calling. His attention to detail, that was usually scattered up, down, and all around, was fixed like flint on the ground in front of him. Luckily, the snow had stopped, and the early frost had given little opportunity for the frozen flakes to accumulate on the ground.

"Over here!" the mouse hollered. He was a few yards away from the found charm.

"What is it, Son?" Cooper asked.

Herbert didn't take his eyes off the ground, and the signs he had found. "Look," he pointed. "There are footprints going into the barn, and horse prints coming out."

"This is a farm, Smarty," Steven mocked.

"But, look," he protested. "The hoof prints are shoed. Farmers don't shoe work horses, the ones that pull plows and grain wagons. They shoe the ones that are hitched to buggies that travel on the roads. Those larger prints, right there, are where her uncle went into the barn looking for her, and there, he's coming out." He pointed to each exhibit. "Those shoed hoof prints have to be the last ones laid down when Silvia left on horseback, sometime late last night, or early this morning."

"Great job, Son," the Sheriff said as he slapped the boy on the back. He raised his hand like a wagon train guide, and rallied everyone to round up the wagons.

Millie smiled and thought, *you really are a good Indian tracker, Little Mouse.* But, like Old Grandfather said, there is more power in not telling everything you know.

Everyone followed Cooper to the bus. "People, focus here. Millie and Herbert have found significant clues."

"Fancy Indian work," Sarah mocked.

Millie said nothing. She studied Herbert, like an insect under one of Mr. Sherlock's lab microscopes. He was so proud he had found a great clue some of his mousiness seemed to have evaporated. There was nothing to be gained by humiliating him. Maybe one day, he would own his heritage, and then he would no longer be Little Mouse. Perhaps Old Grandfather would have a heroic name for him.

"We believe that Silvia rode a horse from the barn, toward the east. Hoof prints confirm that. She had been in Greenville yesterday. We are going to load up, and go over there to see if we can pick up the trail."

"What if the trail ends before we get there? We could pass her," Steven said.

"You're right," Cooper agreed. Then he asked, "What do you suggest?"

"Well . . ."

"What if we search the farmland on both sides of the road, and hope to see a stray horse somewhere?" Millie suggested. "If Silvia was thrown off, the horse hasn't made its way back to the barn on its own."

"Can we ride on the bus with you," Ida pleaded.

"Of course," Miss Hollander agreed. She took Ida's arm and steadied her as she boarded the bus.

The Strausburgers looked up and down the aisle. Kids were everywhere. Many occupied one seat all to themselves. Millie thought Silvia's aunt looked older than she had ever seen her. She jumped up and gave the couple her seat, shoved Steven over, and sat down beside him. She had to say something, but had no idea what words to use.

"She's a smart girl, Mrs. Strausburger," she soothed as she reached over the seat and touched the woman's shoulder.

"I know, Millie, but thank you," Ida whispered.

Millie felt sorry for her. But, she also wondered why Ida hadn't cared about Silvia while she was safe at home in her own room. She said nothing. There is strength in silence, she remembered.

The driver drove only twenty miles per hour as he skimmed along the road going east. Perhaps they would get a clue. All eyes searched left and right and out the front windshield.

The bus crawled along to the edge of Greenville and started to turn past the Greenville Union Cemetery, when someone shouted, "There's a horse in the cemetery."

"Where?" Cooper asked as he scanned the whole area.

"There," Steven added. "Near the entrance."

The driver pulled up to the gates of the huge garden of stones and marble and opened the bus door. Everyone stood up and started to flow into the aisle.

"Stay seated until we know what's going on," Cooper said. "Wilber, will you come with me?"

The two men got off and talked quietly beside the bus. Steven casually stood up and opened his window a crack.

"The horse looks like it's been tied here a long time," Steven heard Cooper say. "Is it yours, Wilber?"

"Yes, that's my Blaze. See the markings on her forehead." He put his hands in his pockets and looked around, acre after acre of plotted-off spaces. "But, where is Silvia?"

"If she is in here, we'll find her, Wilber. You go help Ida, in case she wants to get off the bus. She looks terrible tired."

A dog barked in the distance and the wind blew the last few stubborn dry leaves from the trees. The breeze through the branches created crackling sounds. The students whispered, like they were afraid to talk into the snap and whirl. This was real. Silvia was missing, and the only clue they had stopped at these gates.

Millie looked in the direction of the barking dog and her heart leaped in her chest. Hat-man's truck was parked a short way down the road beside the Cemetery fence. Where was he and where was Silvia? Would they find her before he did?

"All of you students," Cooper started with a whisper, "fan out as you did in the barnyard. Every once in a while, call out her name. She may be unable to move, but might still be able to answer you. Please, be respectful of the graves. Try not to walk on them."

The march across the tree lined lanes and manicured resting places, was more like a dirge than a search party on a mission. Millie couldn't stand the silence of no-hope.

"Silvia," she sang out in a friendly, positive sound. "Beautiful Silvia." Then, she listened. Nothing.

The others picked up on the chant, "Silvia, beautiful Silvia."

Millie heard great sobs behind her. She hoped it was her friend. At least, they could follow the sound.

Sarah came up and whispered, "It's her aunt. It's not Silvia. She seems broken."

Many heard the crying and looked back for a moment. Some of them wiped their own tears from their cheeks and kept their ear tuned to the air.

"Wait! Wait!" Millie heard from behind her. When she and Steven turned, Ida was stumbling after them, gasping and weaving.

Steven darted back to her side and put his arm out for her to lean on. "Mrs. Strausburger, you should not run like that."

Millie hurried to her, afraid the woman would collapse. "There is a bench over there by the path. You need to rest."

"No, no, I think I know where she might be," Ida gasped. "Please, help me."

"You stay here and we'll go," Millie offered.

"No, I have let that poor girl down so many times I will not do it again."

"But, Ma'am," Steven talked gently to her. "She may need help right away."

"Okay, I understand," Ida gave in. "You hurry on and I'll follow."

"But, Ma'am—"

"That's the way it is," she stated flatly and then pointed. "Silvia's parents' graves are way over there, on the far edge of the cemetery. See the large angel statue? They are to the right of that." She stood up, then shooed the two off in that direction. "Run. See if she's there. I'll follow."

"I will walk with her," Sarah offered. "Don't worry, Millie."

They hurried toward the outstretched wings of the heavenly being. As they approached, they saw two figures. One was on the ground and the other one was bent over the limp body.

"Sheriff!" Millie shouted and looked off to her right. The sheriff turned and followed her and Steven as they raced to the spot.

"Silvia!" she called again as she got closer. There was no response.

When they arrived at the spot, the young man in the straw hat was holding Silvia's head in his lap. Blood dripped down her face and onto his pants. His hands were bloody and shaking.

"Wait!" Cooper shouted to Millie and Steven sharply. He raced into the lead and put his hand on his service revolver. "Stand away," he ordered the boy.

"I am holding her, Sir," the young man whispered. His words stuck in his throat.

"Millie," Cooper motioned toward Silvia, "get down there on the ground and hold her head. Be real careful. Make sure you secure her neck. Son," he said to the strange young man, "move over and sit right there." He pointed to a spot on the grass about six feet away. "Steven, make sure he stays there, but don't get close to him. Just let me know if he moves an eyelash. I have to attend to Silvia."

Millie knelt down on the grass and eased Silvia, bleeding and unconscious, onto her lap. That freed the stranger to obey the sheriff. With no thought to herself, Millie smoothed her friend's face. It was dirty and soaked in her own blood. She looked around for something to blot Silvia's bloody eyes. All she saw were broken chunks of cement from the pathway, dirty leaves that had clustered around the base of tombstones, and little else. With the end of her skirt, she wiped Silvia's cheeks.

"I don't have anything clean to touch her eyes," she cried, holding back her own tears as best she could.

"Here," Cooper said as he got out a clean handkerchief from his pocket and gently smoothed away the blood that had gathered in the corners of Silvia's eyes where it had pooled. Then he lifted her wrist carefully and felt for a pulse. "It's there," he smiled with relief.

"Silvia," Millie whispered as the classmates circled around them in silence. "Silvia, we are all here for you."

From the back of the little gathering, one person, shaken and full of shame, pushed her way through. Ida Strausburger, nearly unable to speak, limped forward, "Is she . . .?"

"She's alive, Ida," Cooper assured her. "But she's unconscious."

Ida got closer. Fumbling and unsteady, she crouched near the girl's ear. "Silvia," she sobbed and then cleared her throat again, "I was wrong. I was wrong," she cried. Miss Hollander came to Ida's side, supported her and helped her up.

"Look," Millie gasped, as she watched Silvia's eyes flutter and open slightly. "Oh Silvia, you're back."

Ida threw both hands to her face and prayed a thanksgiving that only a few could hear. "Praise the Lord! Praise the Lord! Thank you, thank you!"

"Welcome back," Cooper said with a grin. "Now Honey, I have to ask you . . . did that young man," he pointed to the one he had parked under Steven's watchful eye. "Did he attack you?"

Silvia turned slightly to see him. "I don't know. I don't know what happened. Who is he? Maybe . . . I don't know." Her voice was weak, but the air was so still around her, everyone could hear.

The kids all turned to charge at him, but Cooper shouted, "Back off. We don't know the facts yet."

"Was it an accident?" Cooper asked again. "Did he hurt you?"

"I . . . I can't remember," she said again.

"You stay right there," he barked angrily at the stranger, "while I figure out how to carry her out of here, and arrest you at the same time."

"I will carry my niece," Wilber stated. He came over and scooped her up, like she was a new kitten, and carried her toward the bus.

The Sheriff went to the young man and shouted, "Stand up!"

"I did nothing!" the hat-man protested.

Cooper jerked him up by the arm, and pushed him in the direction of his squad car. "You're under arrest."

"No, I didn't do anything," the boy cried. When he passed Millie, he pleaded, "I know you. I saw you yesterday. Tell Old Grandfather what has happened. Please . . . tell him!"

13

A Turn of Events

"Well, I'd say you look a little better." Millie squinted as she came into Silvia's hospital room later that day. The drapes were closed and the room was dark, except for a small light above the bed. "But what I really want to know is . . . are you all right?" She patted her hand. "Why is it so dark in here?"

"The light hurts my eyes." Silvia's voice was weak and she kept her eyes closed. Then she opened her lids slightly. "But I'm glad to see you."

"Did you know, that boy who was with you when we found you, was arrested?"

"What boy?" Then she opened her eyes completely, her brow furrowed in pain. "Who are you talking about?"

"There was a young man on the ground, holding your head in his lap, when we found you."

"I don't remember," she said as her voice faded.

"Silvia, when the sheriff asked you if the boy had attacked you, you said, 'I don't know, maybe.' It's important for you to remember."

"But I can't," she said, and closed her eyes again.

"I'll leave and let you sleep." Millie stood and straightened her coat. "But, the young man said something else. He said, 'I saw you yesterday.' He was the young guy in the straw hat." Millie watched Silvia's face to see if there was a reaction. "Then he said, 'Tell Old Grandfather what happened.'"

Tears rolled down Silvia's face, and she turned her head away. "I can't remember."

"I will tell Old Grandfather, if he is still in the teepee," Millie said.

"No!" Silvia pleaded in a strained voice. "Please—"

"But why? That boy could be in a lot of trouble." Millie couldn't understand. She was confused. What surprised her most, she even felt a little angry.

"But, I can't remember," Silvia whispered again.

Millie sat down beside her, reached out and patted her hand. "You rest, Silvia. Sheriff Cooper will be here in a few minutes to take me home. You must be really tired. It's been a long day."

"Millie, I . . ."

"I understand. You're afraid. You don't know what your aunt will say. You don't know if people, like Herbert," she dragged the name out like it was stuck in her throat, "will tease you."

"It's even more than that." She tried to swallow but couldn't. "Would you hand me the water glass?"

"Sure," Millie brought the glass from the side table. Measuring her words, she asked, "It's more than what?"

"I don't know if I want to find the answers. Not because I'm afraid of what people will say. I'm afraid it will change my life." Silvia sipped the water and closed her eyes to the stress and pain of the day.

14

Charles Blackfish and the Patient

"Now Son, you know she's going to remember soon. She's just in shock now," Cooper said, his face grim and serious. He sat straddle-legged on his chair in a small room of the police station in Greenville, facing the boy. Mr. Hat appeared to be about eighteen, though short in stature. "The police here have let me interrogate you as a favor. But, if you don't talk to me . . . believe me, you will talk to them."

The young man's dark hair was braided and hung down his back. His hands were relaxed on his knees, and his eyes remained focused on a knothole in the wood on the other side of the room. He was silent.

"You can give me your name," Cooper coaxed. Nothing. He pounded the table with his fist. "Speak for yourself boy! What is your name?"

The opponent in the war of information did not flinch. He appeared to be calm.

"You said something to one of the girls. You said that you had seen her before and asked her to contact Old Grandfather. Let me help you," he offered. "I will contact your grandfather for you."

The door opened, and a uniformed officer came into the room, yanked back a chair, put one foot on it, and leaned on his knee. "Sheriff Cooper," he said. "I'd like you to meet Charles Blackfish."

"Okay, now we're getting someplace."

Blackfish looked at Cooper and remained silent.

"Well now, thank you. Our Mr. Blackfish has said nothing so far, and I'm afraid I have to get back to Indiana." Cooper stood up as if he were going to leave. "Oh . . . Officer, do you know someone called, Old Grandfather."

The officer's eyes shot from Cooper to Blackfish. "Old Grandfather? He's mostly a legend around here. I have concluded he's a myth. You can't find anyone who'll talk about him. If he's told you anything about Old Grandfather, he's lying."

"I am not lying!" Blackfish threw the words back at the men with bullet force.

Cooper was surprised. The man had said nothing, and then, just the mention of Old Grandfather and the doubt of his existence brought a huge response. There was something about Blackfish, something genuine. But he was found at the scene with Silvia all bloody and unconscious.

He lowered his voice, "Charles, we want to help you, but you will not help yourself. Maybe if you tell us how the girl got hurt, we could work out a deal with the prosecutor."

"But I told you. I don't know how she was hurt. I saw her scarf tied to the horse's saddle horn and I wondered where she had gone. I found her on the ground," Blackfish was firm. He said no more.

"Then, I'll have to hold you for the prosecutor. You can make your plea in court tomorrow morning." The officer grabbed the man's arm, pulled him to his feet, and headed him toward the door.

Cooper saw the look of pain in the young man's eyes. He was not acting. It was something else—innocence? "Blackfish, do you know a lawyer?"

"I have no lawyer. I have no money. I have only Old Grandfather."

"Right . . ." the officer mocked. "Only Indian ghosts."

"I'm not so sure," Cooper whispered.

He grabbed up his hat, headed out of the police station and back to the hospital. He needed to ask Silvia a few questions. The school bus had gone back to Indiana, and he allowed Millie to stay with Silvia. He would take her home.

He drove the few miles to the hospital, parked his car in a reserved-for-police parking space, and walked in. "The Emergency Room is that way, isn't it?" He asked and answered his own question, with a thank-you wave over his shoulder.

He first noticed Millie sitting beside the bed and approached quietly. "Is she sleeping?"

"I don't think so. Her head still hurts, so she has had her eyes closed." She patted her hand and whispered, "Silvia, Sheriff Cooper is here."

Silvia opened her eyes and smiled faintly. "Hi. Do you know where my aunt and uncle are?"

"Your Aunt Ida is resting in the waiting room and Uncle Wilber has gone back with the bus, to bring the car back here. The nurse said you can go home this evening. Be careful bending over. Take things slowly. But . . . you've been awake all afternoon, so they think you're out of the woods."

"Thank goodness," Millie sighed.

"You were worried about me?" Silvia looked surprised.

"Of course. You gave us all quite a scare."

"No one has worried about me, since Momma died," she said sadly.

"Your Aunt Ida was so terrified, your doctor made her rest in one of the waiting room chairs." Cooper explained.

"She was?" Silvia asked with amazement.

"She was," Cooper agreed. "Now, I'd like to ask you a few questions, if you're up to it."

"I don't remember anything," she chimed in again.

"I know — but something might come to you."

Millie got up and sat on the edge of the bed, leaving the chair for the Sheriff. He sat down and twirled his hat in his hands.

"So, we found out that the young man's name is Charles Blackfish. He's Shawnee. Does that name sound familiar to you?" His questions were casually, non-threatening.

Millie watched her friend carefully. She was so guarded. What was going on?

"No," was her single answer. She closed her eyes again. Millie thought she was probably hiding from the truth.

"He didn't say much. Oh . . ." he drew out the question, as if he had just thought about it. "Blackfish asked me to talk to Old Grandfather on his behalf."

Silvia's eyes popped open. She said nothing but shrugged and kept her silence.

Millie opened her mouth to protest, but Silvia gave her a warning look.

"Do you know anyone called Old Grandfather?" the Sheriff asked, and looked from one of the girls to the other.

"I heard a tale about Old Grandfather, that he's a myth," Silvia denied, without lying.

"Yes," Cooper agreed. "I heard that too." He stood up and added, "Well, I'd better get back." Then he looked at the girls seriously; his voice low and measured. "You know, Blackfish will be arraigned before a judge tomorrow morning. The prosecutor believes he attacked you. Then you fell and hit your head. He's in a lot of trouble. He'll need a lawyer."

Tears pooled in Silvia's eyes. "That's sad," she said and said no more.

Cooper hesitated, and then walked out of the room.

"Silvia Wagoner," Millie whispered harshly when she saw that the sheriff was out of earshot. "What's the matter with you?"

"I hit my head. The sheriff said so." She would not look at Millie but turned her face away. She continued to wipe tears from her cheeks with the back on her hand.

"I know you did," she scolded. "But, I saw your expression. I know you remember Old Grandfather. Why did you deny it?"

"I didn't. I said that people say he's a myth." She set her jaw and said no more.

"But, this Charles Blackfish fellow might go to jail," she reminded her sternly.

"So might I, or we, Millie Bryson." Then she lowered her voice to barely a sound. "We stole Aunt Ida's car." She dabbed her eyes again with a small white washcloth she found on her bed tray and added, "And . . . everyone will find out I am one-fourth Shawnee. My father's mother was an Indian. People will tease and bully me. Why do you think Aunt Ida has always tormented me?"

"I am really sorry about your aunt. I agree. She isn't fair or even kind most of the time. Oh, Silvia, what a mess you've gotten us into." Millie shook her head, not knowing what to do or what to say.

"Please, keep my secret, Millie. Please," she begged.

"I'll keep it for this minute when Cooper comes back. Okay? But, Silvia, did Charles Blackfish actually attack you?"

"I cannot remember," she rehearsed, not angry or upset. It was more like a very boring line from a kindergarten play, repeated over and over. But it wasn't pretend.

Mr. and Mrs. Strausburger came in to see Silvia, and Millie let her argument go for then. But, Blackfish's trouble could not be ignored.

"Hi, honey," Ida said as she came in the room to help her niece prepare to go home. "Millie, hi, friend."

Millie couldn't believe what she was hearing. Ida Strausburger didn't talk like that . . . not to anyone. And, the funny part of it was, it sounded like she meant it. "You rest tonight," Millie patted Silvia again. "Miss Hollander said you probably won't be at school tomorrow and not to worry. You and I will do our talks on Monday."

"Wonderful," Ida chimed in. "No, she will not be in school tomorrow. I'm keeping her home. An extra day, plus the weekend, will be just what she needs."

"Aunt Ida, thank you," Silvia stammered. "I didn't know."

"I know," Ida responded. She started to say more and then choked on her words. "I was wrong." Tears gathered in the corners of her eyes. "When you were missing . . . I was so frightened." She reached out and gave her a hug, a genuine gesture of love and caring.

"It looks like you're about ready to leave," the sheriff said as he came back into the all-white hospital room. "Remember, Blackfish is arraigned tomorrow. If you remember anything, be sure to let me know in the morning." He eyed both of the girls. "Are you ready, Millie?"

"Yes. I'll help Silvia get ready to leave, and then I'll get my coat." She ran her fingers over the bedspread and added, "I'll ask Momma to bring me over tomorrow after school." She stopped.

Ida did not permit Silvia to have friends over to their home. She had said, "One fourteen-year-old is enough around here."

"Yes, please do," Ida said eagerly.

"Try to remember, when we're attacked . . . when an arrow comes our way, we must be brave, kind, and honest, Silvia. We can't just duck," Millie said as she tried to focus intently on her friend. But, Silvia only looked away from her, and closed her eyes.

When Silvia was ready, Millie gathered up her coat and belongings. She left with Sheriff Cooper, and Silvia rode home with the Strausburgers.

• • • • •

"I hope she's all right," Millie said as she rode toward the farm. She had almost forgotten the sheriff was driving the car.

"The doctor said she should be fine." He didn't say anything for a while. Then he added, "I'm worried about Charles Blackfish. He's in more trouble than he can handle on his own. He's going to need a lawyer, but he has no money. There's something about him." The car was silent for a moment. "I don't think he did anything, but help Silvia. It's out of my hands now."

Maybe it's not out of mine, Millie thought over and over. Somehow, she would make Silvia remember.

15

A Time for Talking

"Thanks for the ride home," Millie said quickly as she opened the car door in her own barnyard.

"I'll come in. I need . . ."

"That's not necessary, is it?"

"Well, yes it is. I need to talk to your father."

Millie slowed down as she approached the house. The sun had gone down and it was dark. She had forgotten to check the time before she left the hospital.

Millie could smell roast beef when she came into the back porch, and hoped that mashed potatoes went with it. In the kitchen, it looked like the table was nearly ready for supper. Sheriff Cooper was right behind her.

"Sheriff," Bertha acknowledged. She opened the oven door with two hot pads, lifted the roaster and placed it on the stove top. "There's plenty. Can you stay for supper?"

"Thanks Bertha. No. My wife will wonder what happened to me."

"What can we do for you?" she asked as she poured a cup of coffee for Raymond.

"Well now, it's Raymond I need to talk to," he said. Then he changed his mind. "I believe I would like a little coffee, Bertha. It will keep me awake as I drive home."

"Grab a chair and sit for a moment while you drink your java," Raymond offered.

"Thanks," he agreed as he sat down. "Raymond, there's something I have to talk to you about."

"Do we need to go in the other room?"

"No. Millie knows all about it. You and Bertha need to get caught up." He drank a few sips of his coffee, and then added. "You three go right ahead and eat. I know you've worked hard."

After Bertha gave a short blessing, the meat platter and vegetable bowls were passed. Then, Sheriff Cooper began again. "I don't know if you knew that Silvia had been missing."

"Yes, Miss Hollander stopped by to let us know. Glad she was found and that it's all over." She picked at her food and looked at Millie. "We're glad that Millie could be of some help."

"Raymond, there's a young man who needs your help. He has no money, and he's in a lot of trouble."

"Who?"

"He's a Shawnee. The prosecutor says he's being charged with assault. Silvia doesn't say he hurt her. She says she can't remember. But, the prosecutor wants him in jail."

"But, Cooper," he said, "what can I do?"

The Sheriff lowered his voice, as if they were the only ones who would hear. "Raymond, Charles Blackfish desperately needs an attorney. His whole future depends on it." Cooper put the cup to his lips, but only to give the gentle farmer time to catch up to him. "I know you are an attorney, even if you haven't practiced law."

Raymond's fork clattered when it hit the plate. "Cooper, no, I can't. I'm not a lawyer," he protested.

"He really needs your help. He will have to stand in front of the judge, with no one to represent him. His hearing is at 9 a.m."

Cooper finished his coffee, put the cup on the table and stood up. "Well, I have to get home. It's been a long day and I haven't eaten since breakfast." When he got to the door, he put his hat on and said, "Tomorrow morning at 9 a.m. if at all possible." Nothing more was said about the court appearance. He tipped his hat and left.

Millie dropped her fork beside her plate. "I have to be righteous and brave," she sputtered. "I must talk to you." She brushed her hair from her eyes and began. "The truth is . . . . yesterday . . ." she started slowly as she tried to find words that didn't sound disobedient, dishonest, or disquieting to her parents. She inhaled as deeply as she could. She wanted to bring peace to her friend, her parents and to Charles Blackfish.

She closed her eyes, and let out a rapid-fire string of words. "Yesterday, Silvia took her aunt's car, so we could go into Greenville to find information for our Indian papers. And, I remembered to buy that spool of blue thread you needed, Mother. I put it in your sewing basket," she took in another gulp of air. "We went to the library," the words tumbled out, like her childhood marble bag had been dumped on the floor. Bertha and Raymond sat with their mouths open and their eyes wide.

"The librarian helped us locate Great-Great Grandpa James Bryson's farm. We went out there and found the orchard where the Prophet was buried." She prattled on. "Some say Blue Jacket was buried there too, other people say Illinois." She gulped for air again. "Then, we went in the barn and looked around. There was some smoke coming from a clearing in the woods, and Silvia said," she babbled on and on. "Well, Silvia said she had to see Old Grandfather. He was in the trees in a teepee. He told us about James and Rachel Bryson's kindness, and how it was remembered by the Shawnee, and he told Silvia a little about her family. She's Shawnee too," she gasped as she came up for air again.

"Sakes alive, child!" Bertha gasped as she cupped her hands to her mouth. "How? Why?"

"But, I didn't steal the car, Mother. Honest," Millie pleaded.

"Steal the car? No she didn't. Silvia is safe," Raymond stated. "She could only be accused of stealing the car, if her aunt chooses to press charges. Otherwise, it is only borrowing the family car without permission, which would be cause for parental discipline. Again, if her aunt chooses to. If the sheriff arrested every child who disobeyed their family, they'd have to turn the school into a jail."

Millie was stunned. "So . . . Silvia doesn't have to worry about going to prison?" She nearly squealed.

"Of course not," he stated flatly. The decision was made.

"Now, the other thing. Daddy, I don't think Charles Blackfish is guilty of hurting anyone. Silvia said she doesn't remember, but I think she remembers enough to know he's innocent. She just doesn't want anyone to know she is one-fourth Shawnee." Millie leaned over the table, intent on making her father understand how serious it was. "He is going before the judge tomorrow morning."

"Then, I think we'd better get up early," Daddy said. He looked at his plate, sighed deeply and began eating again. "Perhaps tomorrow is the day to speak up."

• • • • •

Morning comes early on a farm, and even earlier if you have a serious mission to accomplish. The cows had to come first. They couldn't wait to be milked.

Raymond put on his blue work jacket and his farm boots and went out into the morning air. His breath stood around his head like his hair was on fire. Maybe it was, with all the stewing and worrying he had done all night long. His memory of the law had to be enough to convince the judge to let the young man go.

"Daddy?" Millie whispered as she came into the barn. Her coat was wrapped tightly around her flannel nightgown. "Please . . . may I go to Greenville with you? I want to be in court this morning. Please."

"Today's a school day, Millie," he reminded her.

115

"I know. But, seeing the court in action is education too," she pleaded. "Please."

"Get ready and eat your breakfast," was his answer. "You need to go to school and tell Miss Hollander what you'll be doing this morning."

"Oh, thank you!" She jumped up and darted toward the door while shouting, "Thank you, thank you." She danced out into the cold morning air.

The house was lit with oil lamps when she went back in. Her mother was in the kitchen. She pumped water into the blue enamel coffee pot and sat it on the back burner. "You're up early," she said as Millie came in.

"Momma," she began her rapid-fire word report. "Daddy said I can go with him to court this morning, if I stop at the school and tell my teacher what's going on. Is that all right with you?"

"Only if I can go, too."

"You want to go to see what happens to Charles Blackfish?"

"To be honest, I want to see your father display his legal knowledge." She smiled with pride as she took some eggs from the icebox. "This may be my only chance," she whispered.

When Raymond came in, the three sat down for their break-of-day meal, but little was said. Millie was anxious about Blackfish's fate. Her father seemed very solemn.

"I know it's a big responsibility, Daddy, standing up for Blackfish. Are you afraid?"

Raymond said nothing, but smiled a little at her. She was afraid that the Indian would be charged with something she believed he didn't do. Maybe, everyone was a little scared about something.

16

The Solicitor

"Daddy, you are a solicitor! It's so exciting," Millie giggled as she rode toward the school with her parents.

"A solicitor?" Raymond asked as he smiled.

"A solicitor is a lawyer who represents someone in a lower court, not a barrister. Just like in my books," she explained as she watched the morning go by outside her window. The sky was bright and blue. She hoped it was a foretelling of the rest of the day.

When they pulled into the school parking lot, they saw that Ida's car was already there. "I hope Silvia is all right," her mother said.

Millie jumped out of the car, ran across the grass that had been lightly dusted with new snow and into the building. She hurried, not ran, into her classroom where students had already began to gather.

"Miss Hollander," she said as she approached the desk, "I'm hoping you'll excuse me from class this morning. I'm going with my parents into Greenville. Daddy is going to represent Charles Blackfish at his arraignment in court."

"Oh, my goodness," the teacher said as she placed both hands on her hips. "Yes, of course. I only wish we could all go. That will be a wonderful learning experience for you. Your father is going to represent him? You'll have a lot to report on Monday."

"Yes, Ma'am," Millie said as she started to hurry out.

Steven Lawrence was just coming in, as Millie got to the classroom door. "What's going on?" he asked as he saw her hurry off in the opposite direction.

"Daddy is going to stand up with Charles Blackfish in court this morning. Gotta run."

Steven waved frantically at Miss Hollander. "I'm going too," he announced and darted out, leaving the teacher flummoxed, but smiling. She waved him off and then dropped her hands on her desk.

"Wait for me," he called after Millie, as they hurried down the stairs.

Near the car, Raymond was talking to Ida Strausburger. Millie couldn't hear what was being said, but Ida's expression was serious.

"What was that all about?" she asked as she hopped into the car with Steven on her heels.

"Good morning, Steven," Raymond acknowledged with a nod.

"He's going along, if that's okay," she asked, but didn't expect a rejection. She slid across on the cold seat, and tucked her coat tightly under her bare legs.

"As long as Miss Hollander said he could," her father answered.

Bertha just smiled and Millie guessed why. Raymond had talked more in the last twenty-four hours than he had in twenty-four days.

The car was silent for the most part. Each rider seemed to be lost in their own thoughts. Finally, Millie asked, "How much farther, Daddy?"

"It's just a mile or so." Then silence.

They came into town and turned onto Broadway. The stores were bright and awake for the morning. Up a few blocks, on the right, between Fourth and Fifth Streets, the court house commanded a large presence on the corner. Raymond parked in the angled spaces out front, and they all got out in silence. He took the lead, as they went up the steps and into the building.

Sheriff Cooper was waiting for Raymond in the hallway. "I've arranged for you to meet with Charles Blackfish in a small conference room," he said as he took him by the arm and led him away. There was no hint of surprise on his face. It was as if he had expected his arrival all along.

Millie, her mother, and Steven sat on long benches that lined the hall outside the court room. Everything echoed in the large rotunda. The passing footsteps on the terrazzo floor sounded like tap shoes from the Vaudeville stage in Dayton. All three sat in their own silence and studied the passing scene in front of them.

Suddenly, Raymond and the Sheriff came clipping down the hall with Blackfish between them. As they approached the double doors of the courtroom, Millie, Bertha, and Steven popped up. All six of them proceeded through the doors without a pause in stride.

"All rise," the bailiff announced.

A balding man with pinched nose spectacles and a long black robe came in, stepped up on the platform, and sat down at the bench. Everyone in the room followed his lead.

"Charles Blackfish," the bailiff read from his list. "The charge is, Felonious Assault," he announced.

"How do you plead?" Judge Benson asked.

"If I may, Judge," Raymond began. "Mr. Blackfish should not plead anything. I don't believe there is a case here, so, there is no cause."

"Judge," the prosecuting attorney objected. "You find cause for the charge, not the defense attorney. So, there has to be a plea of guilty or innocent. I understand Mr. Bryson is new to the court. But, Sir . . . please," the prosecutor protested with arrogance.

"Sir, may I speak?" A voice requested from the back of the room.

"Your Honor," the prosecutor whined. "Must we endure this lack of protocol?"

"Please Sir," Raymond pleaded as he turned to see who had entered. "I know you want the truth to be revealed here. Can the young woman approach the bench?"

"Certainly," the judge responded. Then he addressed the prosecutor. "We want the truth; don't we, Donald?"

"Yes, Sir. But, this Indian—"

"In this court he is not an Indian. He is a citizen," the judge corrected sternly.

"Of his own nation," Donald Mellon complained.

"Well, this morning, we are in a Darke County, Ohio Court Room. So, if it's all right with you, we'll stick with the laws of our county. Will that meet your expectations, Donald?" he asked.

"Of course, Sir," he yielded and sat down.

"No, no, Donald. Please, join us in the well of the court," the judge invited with a sarcastic tone. He motioned for Raymond and the young woman to step forward too. "Not you, Son," he said to Charles.

Millie gasped as she turned to see it was Silvia who was walking down the center aisle of the court room. Millie leaned over to Steven and whispered, "I was hoping she would come."

"She is a brave young lady," Bertha agreed as she smiled at her solicitor husband.

Raymond put his arm around Silvia's shoulder and steadied her. "Sir, this is Silvia Wagoner. She is the young lady Mr. Blackfish is accused of assaulting."

"Well, I hope you are feeling better, Miss Wagoner." The judge was kind to her in spite of the interruption of his court. "Can you add anything to the truth, Miss?"

"Yes, Sir. Yesterday, I told the police I didn't remember what had happened. And, since Charles was found all bloody and kneeling beside me, they thought he had hurt me in some way."

"Your Honor, the courtroom is not the place for an investigation," the prosecutor protested again.

"Truth must be revealed," Raymond protested.

"Well now, I would agree with Mr. Bryson. The courtroom is the place where truth is revealed. Wouldn't you say so, Donald?" The judge grinned at him in a very uncomfortable way.

"Yes, of course Sir, but the time—"

"Are you late for something more important?" the judge mocked again.

"Of course not, Sir," he responded weakly.

"Well, I should think not," the judge snapped. He turned to Silvia and began again, "Now, tell us what you know about this matter."

"During the night and early, yesterday, I was very upset," she began. "I wanted to go to my parents' graves, hoping to find some memory of their love, and how they cherished me and accepted me, no matter what. Feelings I had not felt in such a long time."

Millie looked back at Aunt Ida and Uncle Wilber who had brought Silvia. There was no sign of anger or rejection, just smiles and tears of love.

"She is right, Your Honor," Ida chimed in from the back row. "I am so sorry."

"Your Honor," the prosecutor jumped to his feet. "Is this a court room or a three ring circus?"

"A circus of love," Raymond offered.

"Who are you, Ma'am?" Judge Benson asked.

"I'm Ida Strausburger, her aunt. And she is right. I haven't been caring or fair. I took my grief over losing my only sister, out on her daughter, Silvia. I am so sorry."

"Well, you can make it up to her every day you have with her, Mrs. Strausburger," the judge said kindly.

Silvia wiped her eyes with the handkerchief she pulled from her pocket and explained. "I had tied the horse to the fence at the front gate of the cemetery and walked over to their graves in the dark. I didn't see the broken concrete pieces that had been tossed aside when they were redoing the path to the back of the cemetery. This morning I remembered it all. I tripped on one of the larger piece, fell, and must have struck my head. Charles Blackfish wasn't even around anywhere. I saw no one until they found me in the morning. I opened my eyes and discovered that my head was in his lap."

"Well, well," the judge summed up. "So, Mr. Blackfish was charged solely for making Miss Wagoner more comfortable until daylight and help came."

"But, Your Honor," Mellon protested again. "He was an Indian, walking around in a Christian cemetery."

"I understand," the judge said as he removed his spectacles. "He was arrested for being an Indian."

"Not arrested," Sheriff Cooper stood up and joined in.

Mellon turned and threw up both hands, "Why not have another opinion testified to?"

"He's not testifying," the judge growled, like a black bear in his great robes. "He hasn't been sworn in, and this is not a trial. It is an attempt to get to the bottom of this miscarriage of justice."

"When I questioned Blackfoot," the sheriff explained, "I concluded he had nothing to do with Miss Wagoner's accident.

But the prosecutor wanted to charge him anyway, and he did." Cooper sat down, having said his piece.

"Well," the judge said as he picked up his gavel, "I see no case here — unless you want to protest my finding, Donald." He glared at the man.

"No, Sir. I'm fine with that."

"Well now, we are all relieved," he stated. Everyone in the courtroom chuckled except Donald Mellon.

"I have one question of Mr. Blackfish," the judge looked at the boy with a kind expression. "You don't have to answer. It has been determined that you have done nothing wrong. I just want to know why you started looking for the young lady."

"Your Honor," Charles blushed, "I like Silvia . . . you know . . . I really like her. I saw her father's strip of Shawnee Chief's blanket she wore as a scarf tied to the horse and I had to make sure she was all right."

Silvia looked away and tried to hide her interest in Blackfish by changing the subject. "I didn't know it was a Chief's blanket piece. I just wore it to feel closer to my father. Aunt Ida wouldn't let me wear it." She glanced quickly at Charles and turned red.

"Thank you, Mr. Blackfish." Then he turned to Mr. and Mrs. Strausburger, "You can take your niece home." He looked at them with empathy. "And, I hope you treasure the gem you have."

"Yes, Sir. Thank you." Wilber agreed. Then he put his hand on Silvia's shoulder. "Honey, you can wear your father's scarf anytime you want to." He looked at Ida who smiled and nodded in agreement.

"Sir," Blackfish stood up tall and addressed Wilber, "may I call on Silvia sometime?"

"In a couple of years, we would be happy to have you call on Silvia. As a friend, you can stop by now any time." Wilber shook the young man's hand. "Sometimes she makes taffy on Sunday afternoons."

"This was so fantastic," Steven hooted as he grabbed his jacket. "I had no idea." When Raymond rejoined them, he asked, "Mr. Bryson, will you teach me the law?"

"Sure, but the secret is read, read, read," he smiled as he joined his family.

"Maybe we could practice law together," he suggested to Millie. "Lawrence and Bryson, Attorneys."

"Bryson and Lawrence, Steven. Bryson, then Lawrence," Millie insisted.

17

Greenville on Saturday

"Millie," Bertha called up the stairs on Saturday morning.

"Yes Mother," she bounded down the steps, two treads at a time.

"It's a wonder you don't break your neck." Her mother shook her head and smiled. "Daddy and I are going to do our trading in Greenville this morning. We wondered if you want to ask Steven to go along."

"And, Silvia too?"

"Honey, Silvia just got out of the hospital. She was in court yesterday. I don't know if she is ready to run around town. And I don't know if Ida is ready for her to be out of her sight."

"Isn't that amazing? Mrs. Strausburger had nothing good to say about Silvia. Now, she has nothing bad to say." Millie smoothed her hair in front of the wall mirror in the sitting room.

"Sometimes we don't know how precious a tea cup is until we chip it," her mother said. "Love your loved ones while you can," she added. She went back into the kitchen to finish drying the breakfast dishes.

Later, when the kitchen was polished and the chores were done, they rolled down the lane and out onto the road toward the Strausburger farm.

"Raymond," Bertha suggested, "let's stop at the Lawrence place first. That way, if Steven is still doing chores, we can catch him on the way back to the town road."

Millie heard her mother, but didn't hear. To her thinking, there was nothing more beautiful than a winter day, with the sky so crystal blue you could stitch a party dress from the filmy fabric. Unless, it was almost any other day when she was feeling really happy and content. Today was one of those days.

When they pulled into the Lawrence barnyard, Millie began to look around the out buildings and down the lane for Steven. "There he is," she said.

Raymond rolled down the window. "We're going into Greenville to shop. Millie wants to go back to the James Bryson farm. You can drive, can't you?"

"Sure," he said proudly. Any farm boy could drive a tractor, and in 1925, a car was about the same.

"Would you like to drive Millie out there? And, Silvia too, if she is up to going." Raymond asked as he put the shift into reverse. It was obvious that a decision would have to be made fast.

"I'll tell my folks," he offered, as he turned and ran into the house. "I'm leaving, Mom," Millie heard him yell. He came out with his school jacket under his arm and carrying his everyday boots. He hopped into the car and turned to Millie. "I changed out of my barn jacket and work boots just for the Bryson's," he smiled.

"Good barn perfume is how we make our living, Son," Raymond said.

When they got to the Strausburger farm, Millie ran up on the porch and knocked. Mrs. Strausburger came to the door. "We're going into Greenville to shop. Can Silvia go along?"

"Oh Millie . . . I don't know." Her expression was not mean. She still looked worried.

"Please, Aunt Ida. I feel a lot better. The doctor said the headache might stay for a while but if I'm shopping, I won't have time to think about it."

"I want you to have some fun, Silvia, but—"

"Let her go Ida. Bertha and Raymond will be there," Wilber interrupted.

"Well, I guess." She kissed Silvia on the cheek and helped her get her coat. "I do want you to be happy."

"I know," Silvia smiled. So, the two girls piled in back of the Bryson car with Stephen and headed off to a morning of shopping.

• • • • •

In Greenville, Raymond parked the car in front of the Five and Dime, where they all got out and went in.

"Well, let's see," Bertha began. "Yes, there are still chairs available." She removed her coat and placed it around her shoulders.

The store was full of shoppers and visitors, so the wooden folding chairs near the front door were quickly occupied. From one of those prime locations, Bertha and Raymond would be able to see everyone who came into the store, and get their visiting in, while shopping.

The smell of peanuts and chocolate filled the senses, and shattered any resolve to eat less in the days that would lead up to the great feast day, Thanksgiving. The hardwood floors squeaked. Millie wondered if that was a requirement for city shops.

"Here you are, Steven." Raymond held out his car keys to the boy. "Now, bring the car back in the same condition it was when you drove off."

"I will, Sir," he agreed.

The three were back in the car in record time, Steven and Millie in the front, Silvia in the back. They headed out of town, toward Section nine, Greenville Township.

"Is it better to ride or drive out here, Silvia?" Millie asked.

"Do you drive?" Steven asked.

"Not much," was all Silvia said.

"Did you tell your aunt and uncle?" Millie asked over the seat.

"Yes, and was I surprised. Aunt Ida said, 'If you want to drive, we'll get you a small car. Uncle Wilber can make sure you can handle it.' Can you believe it?"

Millie chuckled. "What shade of black do you want?" Millie teased.

"Maybe they'll buy you a flashy yellow roadster," Steven laughed.

"Don't hold your breath until that happens," Silvia whispered.

"It sounds like you're not ready to trust Aunt Ida yet," Millie suggested.

"I guess not. But I have hope." Silvia's tone rose to a positive level.

Then Millie sputtered with glee. "There it is." She pointed to the orchard and the house. This time however, people were getting out of a car that was parked in the driveway like they had just gotten home. "Oh no," she sighed and then pointed. "Look, there's smoke again."

"Smoke?" Steven looked around the barnyard for evidence of a fire.

"Old Grandfather," Millie whispered, like she didn't want to scare him away.

"Old Grandfather?" Steven mouthed as he searched the farm yard in front of him.

"Can't we just go up to the people and ask if we can walk back to the woods?" Silvia asked.

"But, if they say 'No,' we'll be trespassing, when we do it anyway," Millie answered.

"I have an idea," Steven announced. He pulled into the driveway and whispered, "Follow my lead." He opened the door and limped out. "Hi," he said as he waved at the family.

"Good morning," a man in dress slacks and jacket responded. "What can I do for you? We're expecting company in about an hour."

"Well, my sister here," he pointed to Millie, "has been let out of the State Hospital at Richmond for the day. She is convinced that she left a valuable ruby ring in a little tin box back in your woods. Now, her doctors know that isn't true. But, they thought, if she could go back there to look for it, she'd finally accept that it never happened." He looked from the man to the woman, like he was searching for understanding. He didn't dare look at Millie. She may never look at him again.

"You say she's a little batty?" the wife asked.

"Well, no . . . at least, not anymore. She just needs to prove to herself that the tin box is in her imagination, and she'll be cured."

Millie reached through the open window and pinched Steven on the arm. Rather than hide the attack, Steven used it to further his story.

"Ouch," he squealed. Then he looked back at the family, "Sorry, she pinched me. I told you, she doesn't want her delusions challenged."

The woman stepped back a few steps and shouted at a little boy who had just charged out of the house. "No, Tommy, stay away from the car!"

The man stooped, looked through the windshield and studied Millie from outside. "Is it safe to have her around the place?" He gawked a little more at the "batty" girl on his property. "Well, I don't know," he dragged out.

"Look," Steven offered as he looked at his watch, "it's 10:30. We'll be off the place by 11. How does that sound?"

"Well, I guess," the man said.

His wife added, "Make sure you keep her away from the house."

"Yes, of course." He turned to Millie and smiled, but Millie was not smiling. "Good," he said, "keep your part up."

"How do I keep up an act when I don't know the lines?" she blustered.

"This is my sister's childhood friend, Pamela." He pointed at Silvia. "She will help Gertrude to stay calm."

"That's good . . . I guess," the man said. He watched with wide eyes as the three got out of the car in his barn yard.

"Now, watch your step," Steven cautioned Millie. "She tends to stumble and drool a lot," he explained. He took her by the arm, and Millie nearly jerked his sleeve off.

"I'm fine today, Egbert," she smiled.

"I hope she doesn't start whistling like a mocking bird," he offered apologetically. "She tends to do that, from time to time."

"A mocking bird?" the mister asked.

"Yes, but she has mostly passed that stage."

"I think she's doing really well today, Egbert," Silvia joined in. She came up beside Millie and steadied her other arm.

"You'll have to make sure the gate to the side field is closed and latched. There's a bull out there that can get pretty mean."

"A bull?" Millie gasped.

"It's okay, Gertrude," Steven soothed. Then he said to the man, "She had a really bad experience with a bull, right before we had to hospitalize her."

Millie turned and looked at the man and woman with a wild-eyed stare. "I'm much better now." She let her eyes roll around in her head. If she had had the time to go to the library and had done a little research, she might have known how a "batty" person would act.

The family scrambled into the house and closed the door. Millie heard the latch slide closed.

The three of them hurried down the lane. Millie looked back at the house over her shoulder. "I hope we can finish what we came to do, before the man comes back out with a shotgun."

About half way down the lane to the woods, two angry eyes glared at them from the field off to the left. The massive muscles of the stout animal with the sharp horns were motionless in the field, but only for a moment. Millie, Silvia and Steven were paralyzed in the lane, afraid to move, for fear they would startle the beast, and afraid not to move, for fear the animal would charge.

Suddenly, the bull started to paw at the ground. He lowered his head and prepared to charge. Millie was already "batty," she might as well run frantically down the lane. As she started to move, the bull charged! She screamed, flailed her arms, and flew toward the woods. At least she could climb a tree. The bull out-smarted her. Rather than stop at the fence, he turned and thundered along the thin barbed wire and pounded down the pasture beside her, shaking the ground as he ran.

All three raced the bull to the woods, not knowing if the fence gate was closed or open at the trees. They may have been running into danger, not away from it. When they got to the wood line, Steven stopped up short. There among the trees was Old Grandfather, waiting, smoking his pipe.

Old Grandfather stepped out of the tall oaks and held out his hand, palm facing the bull. The animal stopped and threw its head to the side. He did not move as the three hurried into the shelter of the woods. The trees were so close together, the bull would not have been able to push his way through in pursuit.

Steven said nothing, but followed the girls into the teepee and sat down on the furs. Millie saw his wide, bright eyes scan every inch of the room.

"I used to dream about Indians and their teepees," he said with awe. "I never dreamed I would be able to actually live the dream."

"You are a farm-brave, who has found a second home," Old Grandfather said.

"I think you're right," Steven grinned.

"You would be proud to be an Indian?" Silvia asked, surprised by his enthusiasm.

"Of course," he said, as he caught sight of a bow and quiver lying on a pile of pelts behind the old Indian.

"Then, I was right to come here," Silvia decided. "Old Grandfather, I know you stay here in the woods most of the time." She stopped and proceeded carefully. "Would it be possible for you to come to our school on Monday? Millie and I would like for you to tell the class what we talked about when we were here the last time."

"The wind has told me that you were hurt since last we sat by my fire," Old Grandfather said.

"Yes, Sir," she answered.

"And the trees said you spoke truth for Charles Blackfish," he continued.

"Yes, it was hard. I was afraid I would get into trouble for borrowing Aunt Ida's car," she admitted.

"Borrowed?" he asked.

"The truth is . . . I didn't have her permission to drive it into Greenville that day," she admitted again.

"The truth is all that is real, Little One."

Steven's eyes grew large. "You girls speak like you know this Indian," he said as he shook his head in disbelief.

"We do. This is Old Grandfather," Millie introduced him. "And Sir, this is—"

"Steven Lawrence. Your father is a good farmer. You can learn a lot from him," he said as tobacco smoke swirled around his head.

"How did you . . ." Steven looked at the wisdom in the old man's eyes and added. "Never mind."

Both of the girls smiled a knowing smile.

"You three are not the only ones who visit my teepee," he explained. Then, to Silvia, he added, "You were brave," the old one said to Silvia. "You have a wonderful friend in the Bryson family. They have been our brothers for many generations. Yes, my young friends, I will come." His expression became serious. "What will your classmates say?"

Millie looked at Silvia and back at Old Grandfather. "We don't care anymore," she said. "We will speak truth."

18

The Healing

The boney branches of the willow trees out past the windmill in the Bryson barnyard were blowing hard the next morning. The blades on the mill turned, the limbs in the tree twisted, and Millie wandered if that meant there was change in the air. She hoped so. The last few days had been an adventure, but she wasn't sure if she was ready to relax at the piano in the parlor. Not that she liked racing a bull down a country lane. But, it was exciting to remember the heart-pounding chase.

Christmas would be coming on in a little over four weeks. With Thanksgiving next week, there would be extra cleaning and baking to do at the house. Funny, with everything that had happened she was not ready for life to be normal again.

"Better hurry," her mother called from the back porch, where she sat hulling walnuts. She wore heavy garden gloves that had gotten torn at the top. The stain from the shells could not get through the cloth to her fingers. She pressed on the green, bumpy skin of the walnut with her thumb and removed the nut with a jack knife by peeling off the hull.

"I am hurrying," Millie agreed, as she dashed in a flurry to the wooden porch peg to fetch her coat. She pulled her hat over her head, shoved her hands in the mittens her mother had knitted, grabbed up her books, and darted out of the house.

"Bye, Daddy," she called out as she flew down the lane.

By the time she got to the road, the bus was just pulling to a stop. She hurried on board and swung into the seat beside Steven.

"Do you think he'll come?" Steven asked the minute she hit the cushion.

"Old Grandfather?" she whispered. "I have no idea how he'll get there. But . . . yes, I think he'll come. I don't believe the man would know how to lie." She thought about the possible reaction of the class to his presence, then added, "Don't tell anyone. There could be a reason, beyond his power to change, that could prevent him from being there this morning."

"Saturday was amazing," Steven whispered. "Thanks for letting me go along."

The bus made a couple more stops and then pulled into the school yard. Everyone hurried off like they were anxious to go to school.

Millie smiled, "I think they are more excited about seeing their friends than to learn something new." Suddenly, she thought of Herbert. "I don't think our Mr. Schmidt will ever learn anything."

Steven spotted the principal in the hall and remained on the first floor. Millie walked up the steps.

Upstairs, Silvia waited for her. "I am so nervous." Silvia hung up her coat, and paced the floor. "I know he'll come, but what if the others don't welcome him? What if they're hostile?" She wrung her hands and her voice was strained.

"Who's coming?" Sarah put her hat on the rack above her coat. "Who will be hostile?"

"We have a guest coming today and we don't know if the others will accept him. I'll be honest. They could be mean." Millie looked out the windows toward the east, but saw no one coming. "Isn't it silly," she laughed. "I'm half expecting an Indian on a pony to come riding down the road."

"Now that would be an exciting guest," Sarah laughed.

"It's not silly. I hadn't thought about him getting here any other way." They laughed together.

Sarah joined in the joy of the morning, even though she had no idea what had been planned. She didn't need a reason for her laughter. She was fourteen too.

As the school bell held its tone and rang in their heads, Steven slipped into his seat, huffing as he sat down. "Whew, just made it," he gasped.

"What happened?" Millie put her hand to her mouth and whispered, directing the sound behind her.

"I saw Sheriff Cooper down stairs. I stopped to talk to him."

"Why?"

"Millie, is our class time interfering with your social commitments?" Miss Hollander asked dryly.

"No, Ma'am," she answered. When the teacher turned her back to write something on the blackboard, Millie turned to Steven. "Why?" she mouthed.

"He was near the office. I wanted to make sure he knew that Old Grandfather was coming to school this morning. I didn't want him or Principal Allen to be surprised by his presence."

"Good idea," she whispered.

Miss Hollander didn't even turn around. "Millie, why don't you have the class rise and lead them in the Pledge of Allegiance? You can also lead them in singing the Indiana song, *On the Banks of the Wabash*."

Millie dragged herself out of her seat and put her hand to her heart. Then she protested, "But Miss Hollander, singing and playing the piano do not carry the same talents. I don't really sing."

"Well, isn't it nice that the whole class will be singing with you?" She dusted the chalk dust off her hands and placed her hand over her heart. "Wait, Millie. We're not all standing." She smiled at Herbert and out-stared him into compliance.

"Yes, Ma'am," he agreed. He didn't seem to be belligerent. He just looked tired. "Sorry, I was up all night with a sick horse."

"Hope it's better," she replied. "Okay, Millie."

The class followed her lead and performed their usual class opening exercises. After they shuffled and took their seats again, Miss Hollander turned.

"The history assignment is on the blackboard. After reading the pages, answer the six questions I have written there. Please write the question first, and then answer it. Writing it will help you understand it better, so you know what you're responding to."

She sat down at her desk, pulled some arithmetic papers from the drawer and began entering the grades in the columned grade book. Suddenly, she looked up and gasped.

Everyone turned to see what she saw. There in the doorway stood a man of advanced years with deer skin leggings and shirt, moccasins and a poncho. On his head was a turban with a huge feather inserted through the front. He carried a black overcoat across his arm.

"Bezos," he said.

"Bezos, Old Grandfather," Silvia jumped up and gave the old one a hug. "And a good morning to you all," she laughed.

"Bezos, Old Grandfather," Millie added to the sunny morning, as she came to the front of the class.

"Miss Hollander, I'd like for you to meet, Old Grandfather, a Shawnee chief."

Miss Hollander was stunned. She stood up and extended her hand in greeting. "Welcome." Then she looked at Millie and Silvia. "Girls?"

"We decided," Millie began, "that the best one to give our oral report was a member of the tribe." Then, she added quickly, "We're not getting out of any work. We'll be happy to answer any questions . . . and we have completed our full papers early, so you wouldn't think we were stalling for time."

"Thank you, girls. You have been very responsible." She looked at the Indian and smiled again. She had already smiled a lot that morning, and Millie wondered if she would run out of her good nature any time soon.

"I thought Old Grandfather was a fable," Herbert said.

"Little Mouse, you know better than that," the old chief said.

"What?" some of the class questioned. Others whispered back and forth.

Millie acted as discussion leader. "Everybody, if you have questions, please direct them to Silvia and me." She heard Old Grandfather's mention of the "Mouse" but chose to ignore it. *Strength may come from knowing, not telling*, the old one had said.

"Please, tell the class a little about Tecumseh and the Prophet," Millie directed.

"Tell them why he did what he did," Silvia suggested.

"Do you want to tell them why it is important to you?" Old Grandfather asked.

"Yes" Silvia stated and squared her shoulders. "It's because . . . I am Shawnee, one-fourth."

"Wow," Sarah's eyes widened. "That is amazing."

"How did you get to be a fourth Shawnee?" Jacob grabbed his pencil like someone ready to take dictation.

"I'm one-fourth Indian because my grandmother was Shawnee. Maybe you could choose a different grandmother, Jacob," she joked. "Old Grandfather is a chief of the Shawnee."

The old chief looked out over the class with wise and caring eyes. "When Chief Tecumseh was only about fifteen, his father, Pucksinwah, took him along on a raiding party of a settlers' village. A woman was able to escape from her home with her baby. She ran into the woods and hid in a log. When the warriors had completed their raid and were leaving, a young brave saw the woman and her child, but said nothing. She and her child were spared. That brave was Tecumseh."

"I thought he liked to burn and destroy everything and everyone," Jacob said.

"Let me tell you a story," the old one continued. "There was a time when deer were as plentiful as the leaves on the trees. They leaped through the thick forests and drank from the stream's cradle. The Shawnee used the deer skins for clothing and to cover their teepees. We ate their meat for strength and for winged feet to jump and run. There were many buffalo and game of all kinds. Pelts and furs were used to keep us warm, and line the infant baby boards. Then, the settlers cut down the forest, and the deer herds thinned. The buffalo that were left moved on west. The Shawnee life was never the same. Five of the tribes in the east wanted to stop the fighting, stop the wars.

"Tecumseh's brother, Tenskwatawa, was inspired by the missionaries who preached about love to the tribes. He taught the people to love peace over war, to stop drinking alcohol, to be honest and to stop stealing. He had many followers. He had even predicted that the night would fall on a certain day. It did. It may have been an eclipse of the sun, but the Prophet would have had to know about science to know the day an eclipse was going to happen. When the moon did roll across the sun, and blocked the light, the people were amazed by his ability to know the future. He was so powerful, they called him the Prophet. He wanted the people to stop wandering, to stay in one place, in Prophetstown. They built a council house and established a village.

"Tecumseh was close to his brother, but he could not convince him to preach about saving the Shawnee way of life, by resisting the settlers. Tecumseh wanted to wage more wars, in order to push the settlers out of what had been Indian land, before the treaties were signed. Finally, he thought of a way to discredit his brother."

"Discredit him?" Sarah asked. "Wouldn't he have been able to predict their treachery?"

"Good question, Sarah," Millie encouraged. "Maybe he could not believe that his brother would betray him." She turned to Old Grandfather. "What was their plot?"

[3]"Tecumseh set up a test. He planned to discredit his ability to know events before they happened. One day he asked the Prophet to predict the number of game that the hunters would bring in. The Prophet gave a number. That number was presented to three old men who had been selected to hear the count. Wrapped in his sacred shawl, which was bright red with a blue border, he came in, sat down on a wolf skin and placed the sacred shawl on his head. He reported that the hunting party would bring back a few turkeys and two or three deer.

"Tecumseh had a spy posted at the opening in the tent to hear the prediction. Then, when the old men sent for him, to see if he could predict better than the prophet, he went into the tent in an arrogant and pompous way. He did not sit down out of respect, but stood tall. He announced, 'I see six deer and a load of turkeys.'

"When the hunting party was ready, Tecumseh sent his spy along and told him to bring back six deer and as many turkeys as they could carry, just like he had predicted to the old men. When the old men inspected the catch, they counted six deer and eight turkeys.

"The old men were surprised. They began to believe Tecumseh more than the Prophet."

Millie watched as each of her friends listened with awe. No one smirked at the funny little Indian. She could see admiration begin to show on their faces.

Old Grandfather continued. "The next morning, the old men called for the Prophet. He came into their tent even more humble than before and gathered the sacred shawl around himself more tightly. They took pity on him. The Prophet told them there would be five deer and seven turkeys in the day's hunt. In addition, there would be other small game.

"Again, Tecumseh listened at the opening in the tent. He told his spy to make sure they brought back only one deer and no more. If they happen to kill any other game, like a bear, elk, wolf or panther, they should not bring it into camp. They should wait until the next day, but be sure to let him know the exact count. The hunting party did as they were told.

"When the morning of the third day dawned, the Prophet came into the presence of the old men, sad and humiliated. He crawled on the ground and they could see that some of his hair was gone. This time, they laughed at him, which made the Prophet feel even worse. He told the old ones that the hunt would not be very successful. The hunting party would bring in just two deer and no other game. Then, he got up and left the tent.

"Tecumseh's spy told him he had seen a bear crawl into a log the previous day. He had blocked the hole with another, smaller log and saved it there. When Tecumseh went into the tent to report, he said, 'It is good to understand the ways of the Great Spirit and to be led by him. What more evidence of his power can we have than this, that he enables us to tell in advance what will happen to our benefit in the future? I see four deer, yes, and a bear and turkeys. The deer run into the path of our young men and stand to be captured.'

"Then Tecumseh told them of a dream he had. In the dream, the Prophet had been hung as a false prophet, a traitor and a friend of the white men. When the hunters returned, they bore a bear on a stretcher, four deer and several turkeys. Everyone was very excited. They decided the young men would not go out on a hunt the next day. There would be a feast of bear meet."

Millie looked around the room. Her friends were caught up in the story Old Grandfather told. They were not rejecting his tale. They were touched by the grief the Prophet must have experienced. "Please continue, Old Grandfather."

"The old men put Tecumseh on their shoulders in celebration. However, the spies mocked the Prophet and all the people continued to taunt him. He went into his tent and was very upset all evening. At midnight, he told his wife that he feared for his life, and he was going to the white settlement and ask them to hide him."

"That's awful," Sarah gasped as tears ran down her face. "How could they treat their Prophet like that?"

"Power, Sarah," Millie answered. "Tecumseh wanted power."

Old Grandfather continued. "His wife tried to reassure him but was unable. The Prophet took his tomahawk and knife and snuck out of the village. The people soon heard about it and Tecumseh re-told his dream. His spy ran to the Prophet's tent and asked his wife where her husband was. Neither the wife nor the daughter told where he was, so the spy killed them both."

Some in the class gasped at the fate of the Prophet's family. They sat in sober silence at the re-telling of the fate of one Shawnee who only wanted peace and love.

"When Tecumseh was told of these events," Old Grandfather said with a reverent voice, "he sent a party after the Prophet. The Prophet didn't think he would be pursued during the night and fell asleep about a half mile from the white settlement. Tecumseh had told the raiding party to bring the Prophet back, and if the white village would not give him up, they should kill all the people in the village. The hunting party caught up to the Prophet and dragged him back to the camp."

Old Grandfather looked out the window, as if the story were written on the wind in the trees.

"The Prophet was told he could make a speech. The Prophet rose with a humble and broken heart. He raised his hands to the people and said. 'My conduct is not so bad and so full of mischief as to justify all this suspicion. Some evil spirit seems to have taken hold of me, and compelled me to lie to the old men. And, rather than lie and deceive, I gave up the prophesying, and to avoid the disgrace, I left camp.'"

Old Grandfather continued telling the fate of the good and brave Shawnee. "The Prophet told the people, 'You should have remembered that I have always been a good and true man, and that my nation has always been dear to me and my life has been devoted to it. I had four sons, good and true, who

142

brought much provisions to my tent, enough for us and much to spare, which your children ate. Where now are those four sons? Their bodies are prey to wolves and wild beasts, and their bones bleached on that last disastrous battlefield.'"

Old Grandfather's eyes seemed to be fixed on distant memories. Then he added, "The last battle was our loss to Anthony Wayne on the Maumee River."

Then he continued. "These are the final words the Prophet said to his people. 'My family has been all taken away from me. What have I to live for? You can kill me, as I expect you will, but first I demand to know who has killed my defenseless and innocent wife and daughter. Does no one speak? Are you already ashamed of the deed, so that you hide it? Let the cowardly brute who has performed this deed, acknowledge it. Coward, you dare not say, 'I am the man.'

"The spy now advanced a few inches, and said, 'False prophet, I am the man.'

"Fast as lightening, the Prophet threw his hatchet with perfect aim and power. The spy fell dead. Then the Prophet attacked Tecumseh, but instantly, a worrier struck him from behind and hit him with a heavy club on the side of his head. The Prophet fell, stunned, to the ground. They tied his hands behind his back and Tecumseh yelled out, 'Let him be hanged to that tree.'

"With a piece of buffalo hide around his neck, they hung him to the tree. Then, they walked away.

"Thus is recorded the tragic end of a great man, the Prophet. He did not die as a coward. He knew that Tecumseh had caused his ruin."[3]

One of the girls behind Steven could not control herself. Her tears flowed down her cheeks.

Old Grandfather paused out of respect for those who wished to mourn for a people they didn't even know. Then, he began again. "Toward the evening, things changed. The people remembered the Prophet's speech, and thought of his family, and all the kind acts he had performed. He cured illness with his medicines, shared his food and spirited conversation.

"The Prophet was taken down from the tree, and his property was gathered. Early the next morning, almost the whole tribe accompanied his body to the burial ground at the council house. The sacred place was located on the land that was soon owned by James Bryson and then his son Joseph occupied the ground, where the Prophet's grave remains to this day.

"After many braves were killed by the army who were protecting the settlers, my people realized they had made a mistake. They came to the Prophet's grave to pay their respects. The people realized that his preaching of peace and love and acceptance was right."[a]

"I hadn't heard that story," Elizabeth Packard whispered. Her eyes were big and rimmed in red from crying.

"Remember, not all Indians are warring like Tecumseh, and not all Indians are peaceful, like the Prophet. We are as different as there are stars in the sky, just like you are," Old Grandfather reminded them.

Millie spoke up. "It's all in the Darke County, Ohio History book. That book is in the Greenville Library, just across the state line. All of these lands were part of the Shawnee homeland."[3]

"How would you tie this to Longfellow's poem, Millie?" Miss Hollander asked.

Millie thought for a moment. "Tecumseh didn't listen to the Prophet, just like in Hiawatha. He insisted that the people keep fighting. In fact, he had the Prophet killed. So, most of the Shawnee people vanished from Ohio. The Army marched them along the Trail of Tears, with the other tribes and onto lands many states west."

"That's right, Millie. You got the point of the assignment. Please, continue." Miss Hollander clapped her hands.

Millie smiled and placed her hand on Old Grandfather's shoulder. "There was even a Shawnee tribe called the Loyal Shawnee, because they fought for the Union during the Civil War."

"Did they use bows and arrows and wear blue uniforms?" Jacob scrunched up his face in puzzlement.

"No," the Indian shook his head. "They had U.S. Military issue."

"But, they aren't U.S. citizens, are they?" Alfred Noonan leaned forward on the edge of his desk.

"Where are we citizens then, Noonan?" Herbert blurted out.

"We?" Sarah sat up straight, like a deer sniffing the air.

"Never mind," Herbert slumped down in his seat.

"But, you said *we*." Jacob turned and faced him. "I heard you, Herbert. We all did."

"So," he folded his arms tightly. Then he looked at Old Grandfather and tears threatened his eyes.

"You are Herbert Schmidt," Old Grandfather raised his hands like a blessing.

"Some call me Little Mouse," he choked.

"Why?" Sarah stood up on one leg, with her other knee on her chair.

"Because, I'm not brave." Herbert gritted his teeth. He looked again at the Old Indian. "But, I will be brave today, Old Grandfather." He squared his shoulders and stood up as tall as he could. "I am one-half Shawnee. My mother is a fair skinned Indian."

"Then, from today on, you will be called Standing Tall," the old Indian pronounced, "because you have stood up to claim your people."

"Then, I stand up too," Silvia chimed in. "I am one-fourth Shawnee. Old Grandfather, what is my name?"

He studied the girl then said, "You are Cherished One, because I know your mother and father loved you very much."

"What name would I have?" Millie jumped to her feet.

"You do not have Shawnee blood in your veins, young one." The chief raised his arms and showed his empty palms.

"But, Old Grandfather, the Prophet is buried in my great-great-grandfather's orchard. The Council house stood on Grandpa's land and the adjacent farms to the north. All of that area was Prophetstown. My great-great-grandmother told the story of standing at her kitchen window and seeing a group of Indians gather in her yard and among her apple trees. They were there to honor the Prophet. She respected them and honored their gathering by not interfering in their ceremony."

"Then, why did you not tell your class?" His tone was only for her.

"Because, I was afraid I would be called an Indian-lover, Old Grandfather. I am so sorry." She cleared her throat and wiped her eyes. "I was not brave or honest, and I did not add to the peace of our community. I didn't want to be teased. Now, I want to be respected and free to be all of me."

"I am sorry that my people brought pain and sorrow to some of yours," Old Grandfather spoke with feeling. "But, I am not Tecumseh. I am me. I cannot change history. I owe you nothing and you owe me nothing because of the past. But, we can try to make sure the future is ours."

He placed his arm around Millie to comfort her and to include her. "I claim you as my friend. When you *believe* you are free . . . then you will be."

"Oh, thank you! Can't I have an Indian name too?"

"Millie, you are a child of the Shawnee's good friend, James Bryson. Your name, Bryson, carries much loyalty and strength for the Shawnee. I can find no better name, than to name you Bryson Child. Wear who you are with joy and pride. You are the only Millie Bryson the Great Spirit formed. Live all of who you are."

"Thank you Old Grandfather." Millie hugged the peaceful Chief. "I am Mildred Marie Bryson. In Shawnee, I am proud to be called, Bryson Child and I am an Indian-lover."

References

1. Henry Wadsworth Longfellow (1855). From The Song of Hiawatha – I – The Peace-Pipe

2. Ephesians 6:14-15 (KJV). "Stand therefore, having your loins girded about with truth, and having on the breastplate of righteousness; and your feet shod with the preparation of the gospel of peace."

3. A Biographical History of Darke County Ohio – A compendium of National Biography, (1900) Genealogical and Biographical Record. Lewis Publishing Company. Accessed 11/8/2013.

Difference between the Prophet and Blue Jacket:[a]

There are several accounts of Tecumseh's brother, the Prophet. The History of Darke County gave one account. Some writings said that the Prophet and his brother, Blue Jacket, were two different brothers of Chief Tecumseh. Other stories sometimes interchange the names, the Prophet and Blue Jacket.

One list of Tecumseh's family of origin was written as follows:

> Paternal Grandfather – Wawwaythi also known as Lawpkaway and Loyparcowah
>
> Father – Pucksinwah
>
> Mother – Methoataske
>
> Eldest Brother – Cheesauka sometimes spelled Chiksika or Chiksekau
>
> Second Eldest – Tecumseh
>
> Sister – Tecumpease
>
> (Triplets) First born of the triplets – Sauwaseekau (was killed at the Battle of Fallen Timbers)

Second born triplet – Kumskaukau – is believed to have died in the first year

Third born of the triplets – Lalawethika or Tenskwatawa- the Prophet (Tens-kwa- ta-wa)

Sister – Nehaaeemo

Adopted Brother – Wehyahpihreshnwah (Blue Jacket adopted 1771)

(The folk lore of Blue Jacket actually being a white man named Marmaduke Van Swearingen, who had been captured and adopted by Shawnees in the 1770's, around the time of the American Revolutionary War, has been proven, by DNA, to be untrue.)

It is believed that there was one other sister and another brother

Mohnetohse – First wife of Tecumseh whom he sent back to her parents for neglecting their infant son

Mahyawwekawpawe – First son of Tecumseh

Mamate – Second wife of Tecumseh, who died after childbirth

Naythawaynah (A Panther Seizing Its Prey) – Second son of Tecumseh

Notes

Prologue:

Diversity – the state of having people, who are different races or who have different cultures, in the same group or organization.

Tolerance – willingness to accept feelings, habits, or beliefs that are different from your own

Empowerment – getting the power or ability to do something.

Page 11   In the 1920's, 25% of the population of Indiana lived on farms. In "farm country" – the percentage was much higher. The whole family usually worked in the fields, especially the men and boys. School days were shorter so there would be more daylight hours for farm work. In 1929, when Millie Bryson graduated from high school, graduation day was in April, so there were more months available for farming during the summer.

Since the family worked hard, some students had trouble concentrating at school due to lack of sleep and hard work.

Page 13   jerk – an obnoxious person

Page 16   hack – The hack was a horse drawn school bus or closed wagon. After motorized school buses were put into use, many rural areas still called the student transportation, a hack.

Page 22   Tin Lizzie – a Model T Ford

Page 23   knickers – loose fitting trousers gathered at the knee or calf

Page 23   middy – a white blouse like a Navy midshipman would wear, with a large square collar and dark string tie

Page 35   Young people, in 1925, were taught to respect their elders. If an adult was not Mother or Father, or another family member, they were called Mister or Missus. Since Millie called her father, "Daddy," her mother referred to him as "Daddy" when talking about him to Millie.

Page 40   T-model is another way of saying Model T

Page 41   bloomers – large, loose underwear. Athletic or gym clothes were also bloomers or knickerbockers.

Page 46   jake – okay or great

Page 75   elevator car – The elevator shaft is an open column in a building. The elevator *car* is the enclosed box on which the passengers ride.

Page 76   sundry – several or miscellaneous items

Page 81   Holstein cows – white milk-cows with large black spots

Page 88   bodice – the top part of a dress or blouse

Page 89   Court of Common Pleas – A court to hear civil cases between common citizens. They go to court to make a plea.

There was some discussion among pre-publication readers about students back-talking their teachers in 1925. Some schools and some teachers may have been rigid. But, in some communities, fun and open discussions were allowed in the classroom – even in 1925.

Historical-Fiction

James Bryson was my great-great-great grandfather. He really lived on Section 9, Township 11 (Greenville Township) in Darke County, Ohio. According to the History of the County, the Shawnee spiritual leader, Tecumseh's brother, the Prophet, was really buried in his orchard, where the Shawnee Council House and Prophetstown had once stood. There are conflicting reports that Blue Jacket, another of Tecumseh's brothers, was also buried there. Other reports place Blue Jacket's burial site in Illinois. Some information confused the two brothers, and call Blue Jacket, the Prophet. Whichever is fact; the Prophet was Tecumseh's brother and did have a major influence over the Shawnee people in the Ohio area. He was buried in the orchard which became part of James Bryson's farm.

James Bryson's wife, Rachel Creviston Rush, was one of the first settlers to migrate into Ohio. She came with her parents and her first husband, Henry Rush, who was killed at Fort Rush during the campaign of Harrison. A child of Rachel and Henry Rush was the first white baby born in Darke County.

After her marriage to James Bryson, some stories report that Rachel Bryson actually watched the Indian Ceremonies from the window of her home.

Mildred Bryson Gaines was my mother. She grew up on the Lynn-Bartonia Road in Randolph County Indiana as the only child of Raymond and Bertha Bryson.

Raymond Bryson was a successful farmer in Indiana, and later in Ohio. However, he never studied law as is depicted in this story. His great-grandfather, James Bryson (my great-great-great grandfather), besides farming, held the office of Justice of the Peace, was a county commissioner, served for seven years as associate judge and, in 1893-4, he was a member of the State of Ohio assembly.[1]

I describe this book as a Historical-fiction. "Historic"— because the facts come from historical record. "Fiction"—because Millie and Silvia's story is only a possibility, based on the attitudes, prejudices and folk lore of the time. I was not there, and Millie did not keep a diary of conversations from her day. Her school classmates are composites of the good friends she talked about when she remembered her childhood.

As an only child, she was very close to her mother. When she graduated from high school at age eighteen, she moved to Dayton, Ohio to find a job. She wrote letters home to her parents, my grandparents, nearly every day. I have many of those daily correspondences, and the Millie of *Smoke from Distant Fires*, has the same gumption, curiosity and spirit, as the young, energetic woman in those letters.

We must all live our lives fully, accepting who we were, living who we are, and striving to be a better person every day. Life does not go backward. It only moves forward. History warns us what to watch out for. It cannot be re-written and still speak truth. Live a life of truth.

Doris Gaines Rapp

Other Books by Doris Gaines Rapp

Hiawassee – Child of the Meadow: Doris Gaines Rapp and Marilyn Ann Haun. (Summer 2014) Upper Elementary and All ages. ISBN: 978-0-9915033-1-5 (sc) ISBN:978-0-9915033-2-2 (iBook). It's a Biographic-Fiction of Rachel Meadows, a Cherokee Indian, and the great-great-great-grandmother of Marilyn Ann Haun. Released summer 2014 and available to order from any bookstore or online.

Escape from the Belfry: Doris Gaines Rapp. Y/A and all ages. It's 1945 and Adam Shoemaker's father hasn't returned from the war. His mother is in a tuberculosis hospital. Alone, Adam moves from his family's farm into town to the cold and lonely belfry of the Church on Cranberry Street. But, he is not alone. Spirits that seems to wish ill for everyone, and the good spirit of the belfry also live there. Will he choose the light or the darkness? Order from any bookstore, or online. ISBN: 978-1-4808-0056-4 (sc). Available in eBook form also.

Length of Days – The Age of Silence: Doris Gaines Rapp. Adult and all ages. It's 2112 and the policies of the great uprising in the past are still in place. Christiana and her friends run through the dangerous streets, pursued by the blue guard, as they try to overturn the Length of Days policy. Order from any bookstore or online. ISBN: 978-0-9637200-7-8 (sc). ISBN: 978-0-9637200-4-7 (ebook)

Length of Days – Beyond the Valley: Doris Gaines Rapp. Adults and all ages. It is 2113,Christiana and her friends have escaped the Central Zone and are on the other side of Howard Mountain. They have undertaken the huge task of getting signatures from all of the citizens, to overturn the length of days law. Released: fall of 2014.

Holding on to Sand: William James Rapp and Doris Gaines Rapp. Adult and Y/A. An account of James Rapp's nearly three years in Afghanistan as an International Police Advisor, based on an accumulation of his Facebook posts. Available at www.directbuy books.com. Website: www.dorisgainesrapp.com
Contact:dorisgainesrapp@gmail.com
www.danielshousepublishing.com

You can use this tree to make notes about your own family.

There are several blank pages for additional

Ancestry information,

perhaps even great-great-great grandparents.

Happy family hunting!

My Family Tree

____

Great – Grandfather   **Great – Grandfather**

____

Great – Grandfather   **Great – Grandmother**

____

Great – Grandfather   **Great – Grandfather**

____

Great – Grandmother   **Great – Grandmother**

____

Grandfather   **Grandfather**

____

Grandmother   **Grandmother**

_______________________   _________________

Mother   **Father**

____

Me